STONE DEAD

By

Kelvin I. Jones

CUNNING CRIME BOOKS

 Originally published by Robert Hale, 2006. This new ebook edition first published in 2011

ISBN: 1514670380

Prologue

It was almost dusk by the time Rebecca reached the footpath which led to the old well. Lengthening shadows encircled the hawthorn bushes ahead and a strong odour of damp earth rose to meet her.

She had been here almost exactly a year ago with Paul. She had been happier then. A new place, here, at the end of the world (or so it seemed), nearing the conclusion of her quest. She recalled how they had lain naked in the long grass, hidden in the beech grove and made love that long hot summer afternoon. All that had changed. They were no longer lovers now but friends who kept a discreet distance from each other. She had the shop and the local pagan community. They had sustained her.

Through the ancient trees she could glimpse the outline of the granite stones that formed part of the canopy of the old holy well. Some tattered strips of cloth – clouties as the Cornish called them – fluttered above her in the summer breeze, placed here as a healing ritual.

She shivered. It had grown suddenly cold beneath the trees, which was surprising for the day had been in the upper seventies and somewhat humid. A sudden wind blew up and the branches of the old hawthorn tree danced before her, suddenly animate.

At the entrance to the ruined Celtic chapel, she paused to look back down the path. A full moon had risen in the east, its silver orb brilliant and ivory against the deepening indigo sky.

Unshouldering her bag, she took out a small beeswax candle, lit it and began to descend the lichened steps of the old well. Shafts of sunlight spilled onto the still water beneath her, giving the interior a soft luminescence. She knelt on the lower step and placed the guttering candle in a small stone niche to her left. She had come here to meditate and also for her sister's sake.

After some moments, she opened her eyes, which had grown accustomed to the half-light. From her pocket, she drew out a small female figure made from sheaves of wheat. She kissed it gently, then, after a short invocation to Hecate, leant over to place it on the stone at the base of the well.

Then she saw it. A small feathered body, its glazed yellow eye gleaming in the last of the sunlight. She reached out towards it with her free hand but the small body of the Wren was stiff and cold to the touch. A ribbon of blood spread from its beak. At first, she thought it had been the victim of a predator but when she glimpsed the long steel needle protruding from its side she realized it had been placed there for a reason.

She stood up, extinguished the candle with a shaking hand and made her way back along the shadowed path, breathing fast now, her heart pumping. Someone had been here, to her sacred place, her place of dreams. Someone who knew her. Knew her well.

She pulled the shawl tight about her shoulders and quickened her pace, aware that the wind had risen, presaging the first spots of rain. By the time she reached the car at the roadside she found she was shivering. But it was not cold that made her shiver. It was fear.

Chapter One

At last, the summer had begun. Dorothy looked out of the small window of her converted barn and smiled. A deep azure sky, cloudless save for a few wisps hovering over the distant Scilly Isles, stared back at her. Already she could feel the warmth of the sun on her forearm as she opened the window to let in the still cool, early morning air. She went downstairs, picked her sunglasses from the sideboard where she had left them the previous night in anticipation of this long-awaited summer, slipped into her Clarke's sandals and made her way out into the sunshine.

The footpath from Morvah to Zennor was deserted at this hour save for a lone farm collie that was sniffing around her wheelie bin. She glanced about her and made her way eastwards towards the coastal footpath. Already the sun was hot on her back. To her left the great granite rock stack of Zennor Quoit loomed. It dominated the landscape as if it had been placed here by some giant hand. To her right, the great sweep of the Atlantic Ocean lined the coastline. She reached into her string bag and pulled out an old straw hat she had packed in anticipation of a rare spell of fine weather on this third Cornish holiday.

Ahead, the path wound between two high rock stacks, separated by the dense shadow cast by an oblique sun. She advanced her stride, the dust from the track rising in columns before her. She began to whistle a tune to herself and her spirits began to lift. All thought of her grimy office in Croydon began to slip from her consciousness. At last, she thought, I'm here. Two weeks of radiant sunshine away from the bustle and pollution of suburbia. As Dorothy approached the stack, she caught a glimpse of something red. At first, she thought it was an exotic plant but as she grew closer she saw that it resembled a tuft of human hair. Red hair. A strange unease began to pervade her stomach.

When she got to the stack, she halted and raised her hand to her mouth to stop herself screaming. She began to tremble. Then she turned and fled, dropping her string bag, her face frozen with fear, heading in the direction of the farm at the top of the valley. She did not stop until she reached the blistered door of Owen Davies' farmhouse.

By the time Detective Inspector Robert Lean had arrived, the area had been ribboned in the usual manner and the rocks displayed two uniformed police officers, chatting gently as if they might have been spectators at a football match. By now it was midday and the sun beat down mercilessly out of a clear sky. One of the officers had removed his jacket and was swigging a bottle of still water when he suddenly stood up, replaced his cap and nudged his companion.

'Here he is. The Lean machine.'

The in-joke produced a smile from his colleague. Lean was well known for his lack of humour, robotic demeanour, non-existent eating habits and broad frame.

Lean got out of the car and advanced on them, the two men adjusting their body language as he did so. Ahead he caught a glimpse of Don Hubbard, the pathologist, leaning over an opening in a rock. Lean had not seen Hubbard since the Camborne paedophile ring case last year. He hadn't aged but was noticeably even more corpulent. His white coat and surgical gloves made him resemble some strange white whale. Hubbard looked back and waved.

'Any idea who she is?'

'No, not yet. You'll see why.'

Hubbard was his usual sardonic self, Lean observed. He advanced on the rock.

'Down here, sir, in this crevice.' The uniformed officer pointed.

It was the body of a young woman. She lay with one arm outstretched, her head slumped over her chest. She must have been in her late twenties, Lean surmised. Tanned skin and a shock of long curly red hair were already vivid in the sun's advancing rays. The angle of the body made her appear as if she were a mermaid, cast up by a freak storm. The effect was both surreal and slightly incongruous, Lean thought. He recalled his parents telling him the story of the Mermaid of Zennor, the siren who entrapped the squire's son, Matthew Trewella. The story was well known in these parts.

Hubbard grinned at Lean. His equanimity was never thrown off balance by a mere corpse. Lean noticed a smell, a mixture of tobacco, booze, sweat and strong deodorant, emanating from Hubbard. There was always something unsavoury about the man. He was like some overgrown schoolboy.

'Take a closer look. Most unusual.'

Lean climbed down into the crevice. He felt the gorge rise inside him. Already the flies were clustering around the mouth of the stiffening body. Hopefully, Hubbard would not be much longer.

'Strangled?'

'Naturally dear boy. Probably with a piece of electric flex. In fact, I'd stake my reputation on it.'

Lean could smell last night's whisky on Hubbard's breath. Repulsed, he drew back.

'Nothing else? No clothing?'

'None. Tricky one, eh? Oh. There's this. It may give us a lead.'

Hubbard pointed to a small tattoo on the victim's left thigh. Lean peered. It was an ornate pentagram, much more artistic in its execution than the usual tattooist's work. He noticed it had been inverted. Although Lean was staring at a corpse, he felt there was something unutterably beautiful about the body of this unknown woman.

'What do you make of it?'

Hubbard snorted.

'Nothing to confirm her identity. Maybe she was a hippy or a new ager. Who knows?'

'Any sign of sexual interference?'

'Nothing obvious. You'll have to wait for that. As you usually do, old son.'

Lean turned, irritated by Hubbard's patronizing manner. Two men in white suits were wheeling a trolley out of the back of the van. On it was the shiny black bag, already unzipped, ready to receive the forlorn body of the mermaid. He thought of the pale, beautiful corpse being subjected to Hubbard's cruel knife. Somehow it was an appalling, objectionable thought.

'How did she get here? Car perhaps.'

'There's possibly more than one person involved. It's at least a hundred yards from the road.'

'No sign of footprints.'

'None. Whoever came here, covered over their tracks. In my view, it's not a crime of impulse. She was meant to be found.'

Lean did not reply to Hubbard's observations. Instead, he leaned against the rock and watched the men lifting the mermaid into the black sack, reflecting on how she had come to this forlorn end. He took a packet of cigarettes from his shirt pocket and lit one.

For the third time that morning John Bottrell stirred from his sleep, sat up in bed, and grasped his head. He reached for the glass on his bedside table, took a swig of water and stared out of the window at the advancing sunshine. The air smelt of fresh mown hay, but for the moment it was beyond his appreciation.

Swinging his legs out of bed, he changed quickly out of his pyjamas and reached into his overnight bag for a fresh pair of underpants. Then he sat on the edge of the bed, nauseous, musing and listening to Bob's wife Hazel, moving about in the kitchen beneath him. He could smell the strong odour of bacon as it drifted upstairs into his garret bedroom. For a moment memories of similar sunny days spent here in Cornwall with his wife Frances slipped back into his memory, but the recollection was so painful, he drove it away. For months he had thought of nothing else but the road accident and his own terrible inattention that had indirectly caused her death. That's why I'm here, he thought to himself. To forget. No, not forget. Never that. But to ease the pain. To ease the unbearable pain of his loss.

Hazel was calling him, telling him his breakfast was ready. He didn't hear Bob's voice so he guessed that he had been called out early. As he slipped into a fresh shirt he tried to recall last night's recurring dream. It was almost too distant to recollect now, but he thought that it was the same dream he had dreamt before, about a week ago. He remembered a young woman with red hair. She had been struggling with a man with dark hair, but the man's face had not been visible in the dream. Only the girl's face, tear stained and tortured. She had been pleading with the man to set her free but the man did not speak. That was what had made the dream so sinister.

He had had dreams before of course. In fact, he had always had them. The night visitors he had called them when he was a teenager. That was when they had started. And they'd continued all through his formative years. Even when he was in the Met. Of course, he told no one of them – no one, that is, except Frances. She had told him that he was psychic. It relieved him to hear her say that because for years he had thought he was touched. The odd thing about the dreams was that they appeared either to prevision future events or describe things that had happened in the past. The trouble was he could never be absolutely sure. At one stage in his career he kept a diary and was able to match what he saw in his dreams with real events. On one remarkable occasion he had been able to see the execution of a robbery before it took place. He reported both the time and place to his colleagues in the Met on the pretence that he had received a 'tip off'. It had led to a result. But he never revealed the real source of his knowledge.

He made his way downstairs into the large living and breakfast room which Robert and Hazel had converted from an old barn some years ago. When they had first started the conversion Bob had been a mere DC. Now he had reached the exalted plane of an inspector. But that hadn't altered their relationship. They had been friends from school and although John had moved away in order to carve out a career for himself in London, Bob and Hazel had always remained his friends. When Frances had been killed they had been the first to offer him comfort and solace and he had accepted their invitation to stay with them in the cottage at Zennor without question. He had been signed off sick for at least six weeks and told that he must not return until he had controlled his excessive drinking.

'The bacon's done. Hope you like it crispy.'

Hazel smiled at him, her long dark hair falling luxuriantly about her shoulders. She was wearing a short T-shirt which failed to cover her midriff and there was a smell of freshly cut flowers about her. John recalled that Frances used that same perfume. It had been one he'd bought for her from the Body Shop.

'Bob at work already?'

'He had an early call – about seven. I get used to it I'm afraid. You know the routine. It sounded important so I guess he won't be back till much later. Can't tell you what time we'll be having dinner. Thought I might go into St Just and check out that new gallery that's just opened. Care to join me?'

John bit into his bacon and nodded in the affirmative.

'This is delicious.'

He was about to say: 'Just like Frances used to fry bacon', but then he caught himself and resumed eating his breakfast.

The journey to St Just took them via the coastal route. Hazel sat behind the wheel of the big Volvo and adjusted the car radio waveband. As she hummed to an Elton John tune, Bottrell studied the scenery. The giant rock stack of Carn Kenidjack rose and fell as the car sped onwards, enshrouded by a ribbon of mist. To their right the great rock fortress of Gurnard's Head appeared, looking like a huge granite jigsaw. Here and there, isolated cottages broke the long lines of the green summer landscape.

John fell into a reverie. He recalled the autumn holiday he had spent here with Frances years ago. They had rented a cottage on the moors near Ding Dong mine and walked for miles along the old church paths. That was how they had chanced upon Zennor. Inside the small church at the end of the village they had come across the ancient bench end in the lady chapel with its curious mermaid carving. The great age of the church and the brooding nature of the surrounding landscape had impressed them both. They had been told by friends that Zennor was an enchanting place but its strong primeval atmosphere told them otherwise. It had always felt like it was a gateway to the other world.

It was in Zennor that they had first come across Bob Lean. Regulars at the Tinners Arms pub, Bob and Hazel had discovered the unlikely connection that Bottrell had been educated in the same city as Bob (Rochester) and that they had trod the same London streets in their younger days. Bob had stayed in the Met only six years before turning to his native Cornwall, but John had remained to climb the promotion ladder until he had reached the exalted heights of Detective Inspector. Then had come the crash and his subsequent breakdown.

Suddenly the car veered to the left to avoid an oncoming tractor. Bottrell gripped the seat and drew a deep breath. Ever since the accident, the sense of extreme terror had never quite left him. As an advanced driver, he had learned to deal with the most hazardous of road conditions, yet he had been unable to keep his concentration on that fateful night. Returning home after a long trip to Frances' parents in Eastbourne, he had allowed himself to doze momentarily at the wheel of the Mercedes. When he looked up, he heard his wife's screams as the car left the motorway and hurtled down a steep slope, crashing broadside into a concrete pillar on the way down. He would never forget the sight of his wife's battered face as he strove to release himself from the wreckage. Her beautiful blue eyes stared imploringly at him as he struggled to stem the blood from the deep arterial wound in her neck. In his dreams those eyes still haunted him.

By the time his call on the mobile had summoned the emergency services, she had stopped breathing and her body lay in the seat like a crumpled doll.

It was this memory which always returned to him when visiting scenes of murder. Once he could cope with it but now he found it difficult to bear. He thought of his fictional hero, Sherlock Holmes, and the comment someone had made about the great detective after his escape from the Reichenbach Falls in Switzerland: 'He was never quite the same man afterwards.'

Suddenly Bottrell was aware of Hazel speaking to him and the car radio announcing news of a murder.

'What do you think?'

'Sorry, in a dream. I wasn't listening.'

'About the murdered girl. They found her body on the coastal footpath.'

'Oh right.' Bottrell eased himself forward in the seat, wishing that he could light his pipe. An absurd thought, since Hazel was a non-smoker. He recalled something about the discovery on the local radio earlier that morning.

'They've just put out an appeal on the radio for anyone who might have known her to contact the police,' Hazel continued.

'When was this? Where exactly on the coastal path?'

'Early this morning. Near Zennor. A tourist discovered her among the rocks. They're searching the area for her clothes.'

Bottrell pictured the body of a young woman lying among the rocks. A sex attacker most likely. That would be it. He reached into his side pocket and felt the bowl of his briar there, nestled like an old friend, waiting to comfort him.

'I suppose Bob will be on that one. I should delay dinner if I were you, Hazel.'

'I guess so.'

'In which case we'd better make the most of it.'

Bottrell relapsed into a grim silence. He was imagining the girl on the cliff again. Somehow he imagined that she would be naked. Why did he think that? He wasn't sure. He half closed his eyes, shutting out the winding coastal road. He was recalling another part of his dream of the night before. He could see the girl more clearly now. Before, he had pictured her in a room with long gothic windows where there were candles burning, although he was unable to see their colours. At one point there was another woman and two men with her in the room. The girl appeared to have red hair and somewhat rounded features. She was laughing a lot. Then suddenly the man and the woman left and she was alone with this man whose face Bottrell could not see in the shadowed room. At one point he had been referring the woman to a large book that was placed on a round table in front of them. He could not see it clearly but it was ancient and leather-bound. After some while, the woman became somewhat agitated and stood up. The man approached her and delivered a cruel blow to the side of her head. She fell, weeping. The rest of this section of the dream was muddled and unclear. The dream shifted in and out of his consciousness. It was like being on a roller coaster. At times he could see faces, hear voices as clear as a bell. Yet at moments it was like viewing everything through a piece of opaque glass. At other times events even appeared to transpose themselves so that he quite often saw the same scene being enacted by different people.

It was strange how often the pieces of these dreams seemed to jigsaw themselves together over a period of time. He was never able to get the whole picture as he would if he were constructing a story. It had always worked this way, even when he was a child.

He felt it must be the same woman because he remembered in the second sequence that her body had the texture of alabaster and he had been struck by the beauty of her smooth white flesh. She was most definitely dead. It was this dream which he had woken from and not been able to recall earlier that morning. It explained his sluggishness at breakfast and his unwillingness to communicate. When the dreams came, it was as if they closed off part of his waking mind, captured part of his soul. And when he recalled the dream he was liberated from a state of tension.

'Not long now,' Hazel assured him, aware of the silence which had fallen between them. Since the death of Frances, she had found his moodiness difficult to deal with. John had always been the more introspective partner but now he was subject to fits of profound melancholy. Since his arrival in Cornwall, they had found it difficult to engage him in conservation.

He stared at the ruined mining stacks on his right and the tiny art gallery nestled in the Tregeseal Valley, finding it difficult to obliterate the image of the young woman's body from his consciousness. Hazel changed gear badly and the car heaved its way up the hill to the outskirts of the old mining town. Although they had left in brilliant sunshine, here at St Just long wreaths of mist had already gathered and settled in the uncompromising granite streets.

While Hazel wandered into the town's supermarket, Bottrell reached for his Irish briar, plugged it with a sweet smoking mixture, lit it and strolled into the market square. A thin ribbon of pungent tobacco smoke wafted skywards as he gazed unseeingly at the shop windows. The first was a small hairdresser's where a young woman of ample bosom and broad arms was putting the finishing touches to a female customer dressed in tweeds. Next door, a gift shop displayed a variety of resin cast Cornish piskies and second-hand bric-a-brac.

At the third shop front Bottrell paused, momentarily plucking his pipe from his lips. Behind the window was an attractively displayed selection of tarot card packs, a scrying mirror with a polished copper frame, two books by Aleister Crowley and a long dagger, termed by occultists an athame. The items lay on a rich green velvet cloth at the top of which hung a sign in Gothic lettering. The legend read: 'The Moon Stallion. Magical books and products.' Although two miniature spotlights illuminated the window display, the shop appeared to be closed. He peered in but there was no sign of anyone about, despite the fact that it was midday on a Tuesday in July at the height of the tourist season. Suddenly aware that someone was standing behind him, he turned quickly. A pale young man with penetrating dark eyes stared back, a slightly anxious expression on his face.

'Not open yet?'

'No indeed,' Bottrell replied, replacing his pipe between his lips and scanning the man's face intently.

'Huh.'

He gave Bottrell a darting glance, then turned back in the direction of the telephone box where he proceeded to make a call. Bottrell drew on his pipe and let the smoke curl through his nostrils. He sat on a bench in the middle of the square and waited for Hazel to appear. A moment later she emerged, clutching three full bags of shopping.

'Time for a coffee before we head back?' He nodded, knocking out the bowl of his pipe on the bench end, and pointing to the shop.

'Oh, the Pagan shop. It's only been there a year or so. Not very popular with the locals. Especially the Methodists. Although it has quite a following among the converted. There are quite a lot of alternative types in the area.'

'Yes, I can imagine.' Bottrell commented, dryly.

They made their way across the square into a small café, empty save for two young men smoking incessantly over their coffee and a tall blonde woman, engaged in an avid exchange with the owner.

'I can't imagine why she isn't open,' she was saying. 'I only phoned her last night. She said she'd open for a couple of hours and would I do the midday shift.'

Bottrell was listening half-heartedly to her, wishing he hadn't put his pipe out so readily.

'Maybe she's overslept,' the proprietor offered. 'Incidentally, I saw Paul just now outside the shop.'

At this point, he caught Hazel's eye and terminated the conversation. Bottrell looked across at the woman who seemed to be agitated. She had short fair hair and wore an unusual pair of silver earrings, showing a crescent moon. Her face was unusual, high cheekbones and clear blue eyes, the lips firm and rather full. She was of athletic build and had good muscle tone, he noticed. She reminded him of a painting he had once seen by one of the Pre-Raphaelites – Rossetti, perhaps – he couldn't remember. He knew that if he continued staring at her she might think him rude, but he was somehow unable to take his eyes off her. The fact was he found her extraordinarily attractive. She glanced momentarily at Bottrell and turned to leave.

'Well, I'd better go back and give it up as a bad job. See you,' she said.

Bottrell reached for his pipe and dressed it with tobacco, rummaging in his jacket pocket for his lighter. Hazel sighed, gazing at him in disbelief.

The incident room at Camborne was a Portakabin at the back of the main headquarters. Since it consisted of plasterboard walls and large, metal-framed windows, the temperature inside had already risen to an uncomfortable 80 degrees. Lean had borrowed three tabletop fans from his main office but even with these going at full blast, it was still extraordinarily hot and sticky. The bottle of still water which had lain on Lean's desk since his arrival just past midday was now unpleasantly tepid. Nevertheless, he took a swig from it and watched as DC Robertson proceeded to map-pin the Ordnance Survey sheet on the display board opposite. Then he stood up and made his way over to where Robertson was working. To the left of the map were a series of photographs of the body of the unidentified woman.

'Well, what do you make of it?' asked Lean, peering at him intently.

'How do you mean, sir?' asked Robertson. He was always nervous when Lean asked direct questions of this sort. He had learned to be evasive with his superiors. It was the best policy.

'The location, what do you make of it?'

'Someone who wanted to see his handiwork appreciated?' Robertson ventured, avoiding his glance.

'Something like that. And not a random act, either. Any luck finding the clothes?'

Robertson shook his head.

'Nothing yet, sir. We're widening the fingertip search.'

'What about door to door enquiries?'

'Uniformed have completed this area so far,' he commented, pointing to the map. Lean peered at an area north of the coastal path.

'Nothing yet, then?'

''Fraid not, sir.'

'What about the pub here?' he inquired, pointing to the southwest edge of the map. 'Has anyone interviewed the landlord yet? Checked which customers were drinking there last night?'

'It's in progress, sir. PC Symons and WPC Blaise are on to it.'

'Let me know the minute anything comes up. What about the radio appeal?'

'Put one out this morning. Still waiting for feedback.'

'I see.'

Lean sighed. His face a picture of exasperation. A trickle of sweat began to weave its way down his shirt collar. He doesn't really see at all, Robertson thought.

'Why can't we open this window?' Lean jabbed with his forefinger.

'Stuck I'm afraid.'

'Haven't you got a screwdriver or something?'

Robertson rummaged in a drawer and brought out a screwdriver. Get off my back, he thought to himself. And find your own screwdriver. A moment later a blast of cooler air blew across Lean's perspiring face. He sat back in the comfortable office chair and allowed himself a brief moment of relaxation. The office door opened and a WPC entered, accompanied by a tall young woman with short fair hair. Lean turned to examine the stranger. Although casually dressed in blue jeans and a worn T-shirt bearing the logo 'Glastonbury 2000', the young woman had an air of prepossessing intelligence about her. She was also strikingly attractive, it occurred to him. High cheekbones, deep blue eyes and a frame which looked as if she had worked out at some time.

'This is Ms Horrocks,' announced the WPC. 'She thinks she may know who our murder victim is.'

Lean proffered her a chair.

By 3 p.m. the temperature in the portakabin had begun to fall. Although Lean's back and armpits displayed a broad band of sweat through his blue shirt, and his tie had been consigned to the desk drawer, he was a much happier man. Anne Horrocks had moved to the other side of the incident room and was making a detailed statement in the presence of WPC Horner. After that, he would take her to the morgue for what he hoped would prove to be a positive identification.

From the photograph of the victim's face, she seemed convinced that the 'mermaid' (as he had privately begun to term her), was one

Rebecca Wearne from Penzance. She had told Lean that she and Rebecca were friends. They had met socially through a local Earth Mysteries group a few months ago. Anne had been working part-time for her in the occult bookshop in St Just which Rebecca and her former partner Paul had set up a year ago. Lean interrogated her closely about Paul. It turned out that whilst they were still acquainted, they were no longer lovers since Paul's drinking problem had worsened. Apparently, Anne had been around to the shop that morning only to find that it was deserted. Paul had also visited the shop, though she did not know why. She had heard the appeal on the radio and decided that Rebecca's disappearance was too much of a coincidence.

When he had finished speaking to Anne, Lean decided to run a check on Paul Powell. He was agreeably surprised to discover that CRO had a trace of him and he had already appeared before the local magistrates on two separate charges: one for a possession of a small amount of cannabis, the other, a more serious charge of GBH, following a fracas outside a nightclub in Penzance. Clearly then, the young man in question had violent tendencies.

As Anne was completing her statement with the WPC, DC Robertson turned to the incident room bearing a small piece of paper.

'Thought you'd like to see this, sir.' Lean glanced at its contents.

'Well done, Robertson, excellent.'

'WPC Blaise actually sir.'

Robertson enjoyed needling his superior with small details. It helped even up the score.

'Tell her I'm grateful.'

The note explained that a white Sierra had been seen parked in a narrow layby between Zennor and Morvah by one of the regulars at the pub late last night. The farmer in question had been sober enough to recall the first part of the licence plate number. The number tallied with a car owned by Powell.

'See that Powell's brought in for questioning. We'll see what he has to say. No, better still, I'll do it myself.'

Robertson nodded and, casting a glance in Anne Horrocks's direction, left the Portakabin. Lean stood up and went over to the WPC's desk.

'Finished?'

'Yes, sir. All done.'

Lean sat down opposite Anne and managed a smile. He noted that she was an attractive young woman with good bone structure. She was wearing a subtle perfume, a faint smell of lilac. Her left arm, which was extended on the table in front of him, was tanned and muscular. She probably works out, he thought.

'Tell me, Anne, this boyfriend of Rebecca's. Would you say he ever showed violent tendencies towards her?'

Anne looked thoughtful.

'Well, they did fight. Rebecca was a fairly feisty character.'

'When she knew Paul – did she have other relationships? Other men?'

'She never talked much about that sort of thing. She was a fairly private person.'

'What about her other friends – acquaintances? People she met through the shop for example? Did you know any of them?'

Anne appeared to hesitate, clearly she was holding something back. A uniformed policeman entered.

'Car's ready, sir.'

'OK. We'll talk again perhaps. When we've got this over with.'

He stood up to go and the smell was strong in the airless room. Lilies. The flowers of death. He wondered what this young woman's relationship was with Rebecca Wearne. A *ménage à trois*, perhaps?

The morgue consisted of a long room, banked on both sides by a series of steel cabinets. The room smelled of formaldehyde and was lit by three uncompromising neon strips. Michael, the attendant, stood by no. 26, ready to oblige.

'OK?'

Anne nodded. The WPC touched her hand lightly in a simple act of reassurance. The attendant unzipped the bag so that Rebecca's head and shoulders were visible.

'Yes, it's Rebecca all right.'

After they had returned to the cottage, Bottrell took a can of lager from the well-stocked fridge and drank it straight down. Then he went upstairs and, taking a half-bottle of Irish malt from his suitcase, poured a good measure into a glass and swiftly drained it. Sitting on the edge of the bed, he stared out of the window. Already long shadows gave the rocks along the coastline the appearance of small hunched figures, gathered in silence, as if waiting for the approach of sunset. It was already 6 p.m. but his friend had not yet returned. At 6.15 Bottrell heard the telephone ring downstairs and he knew it would be Lean informing Hazel he would shortly be home. His interest in the matter began to wane as the honey-coloured liquid warmed his stomach. He lay back on the pillow and allowed his mind to drift. He recalled the shop in St Just and the strange, anxious young man who had interrupted his reverie. Then he must have lost consciousness for a while. When he came to, he could hear Hazel calling to him and the sound of Bob's voice below. But they seemed so far away that he did not wish to leave his drowsy state.

Although much was indistinct, he could see the room with the gothic windows more clearly than before. He noticed that the candles were alight and that they had been placed in a circle. What he had not remembered from before was that the candles were black. This was certainly a different occasion, though, for the young woman was lying on her back in the circle and this time she appeared to be naked. He was convinced that the figure who kneeled before her and who seemed to be intoning from the large leather-bound book was the man he had seen in the previous dream, although again he could not see his face. The figure moved to the four points of the circle and then back to the prostrate woman. Then he leant over her, his cloak enfolding her, and began to kiss her, each time muttering something.

When Bottrell awoke from the dream he was unable to recall the name of the woman.

Chapter Two

He took the road from the Nancledra to Zennor. It was a quiet route, rarely used by tourists. He knew these roads like the back of his hand and had become well known among his small circle of friends for his ability to dodge the police and the grey MAFF land rovers. The road snaked ahead of him, dark clumps of trees on the horizon standing like sentinels. At this time of the night, the Penwith moorland was other-worldly, a place of ancient secrets where it was unwise to linger. Behind the wheel and the headlights he was safe, cocooned in his metallic shell, but he would not have dared to make this journey on foot without a companion. He preferred to work alone. Not because of any arrogance on his part. He was simply more successful as a solo operative. Leafleting and mass protests were fine but there was nothing so effective as direct action. In the boot of his car he kept a torch and a balaclava hat so that his forays could be spontaneously executed.

Tonight's expedition had come about as the result of a tip-off from a friend in the movement who lived in Penzance. The telephone tree was the principal method by which the members of the group organized such events. They worked always at night when they knew they would be far less conspicuous.

It was just as well that he was familiar with the route, for by now the only lights visible came from a few distant ships along the horizon line. Elsewhere the cloud-racked night sky seemed to be utterly impenetrable. When he hit the Zennor coast road, he drove on for half a mile, then turned down a short track and parked in a lay-by. Noiselessly, he raised the boot and brought out a small black bag. He donned the balaclava, locked the car and waited a few minutes, allowing his eyes to adjust to the darkness.

He stood listening to the sounds of the night. Towards the black rocks on the hillside he heard an owl hoot.

It was at times like this, when he was utterly alone, that he most enjoyed his work. By now his eyes had adjusted and he could make out the path to his left. At the end of the path was a stile. He made his way along the track and climbed over it, watchful and alert. Since he was now off the footpath and on private land, it was in his interest not to be discovered.

He had been told that the traps were beside a small culvert which lay just below the farm. He had decided to approach it from the west side since he would be less conspicuous, but that meant pushing through briars and gorse. He took a machete from the bag looped over his shoulder and began hacking at the obstructions that blocked his path. He was glad he had decided to wear a pair of leather gloves. After a while, he had gained some twelve yards and was in sight of the culvert. Now that he was beneath the edge of the hill and beyond sight of the farm buildings, he flicked on the small high-intensity torch and panned it across the landscape. On the other side of the stream, he could make out five or six steel traps, tucked into the side of the hill.

Flicking off the torch, he knelt down and drew a long screwdriver from the bag. Then he waded across the stream. The ice cold waters closed about his feet, invading his boots. He wished he had worn wellingtons. Reaching the other side, he crouched and began to insert the screwdriver into the opening of the first badger trap. There was a sharp metallic snap as the door clicked fast. Because he was experienced at his work, he was able to withdraw the blade of the screwdriver quickly. If he had not done so it would have been trapped inside. After a few minutes he had worked his way through the five traps, immobilizing each one.

As he was completing this task, he suddenly pivoted round, his heart pumping. Then he began to laugh noiselessly. Over the edge of the hill he could see a dark body moving slowly. It was a badger.

He kept perfectly still as the animal began to sniff the air, picking up his scent. He had no doubt that the creature had been attracted by the bait left in the cages, but now it had picked up the man scent, it was in two minds whether to continue. In the darkness to which his eyes had now become accustomed, he could see the great head, rotating slightly as the creature deliberated whether to continue on its route to the culvert. At last, it came to its senses and plodded over the hill's edge.

Replacing the screwdriver in his bag, he braved the stream and retraced his steps back through the bracken. On the other side of the field a long shaft of yellow light pierced the darkness. He stopped, crouched down, and then slipped back into the shadows, careful to skirt the edge of the field. The cold in his feet had crept into his legs now and he hastened his step, anxious to regain the path. In the distance he was aware of a number of car headlights arcing across the ink-black landscape. They were probably late night revellers returning home but he could not be absolutely sure. Even though this was a remote district, there was always the risk of the occasional police patrol car and with the present badger cull operation; the police had increased their vigilance. At last, he reached the car. Careful to conceal the bag in the boot, he quickly slid into the front seat and turned on the ignition. The car slid forward out of the lay-by. He pushed it into third gear, keeping the revs low. Anxious to avoid drawing attention to himself, he did not switch on the headlights until he was at least a half-mile in the direction of Nancledra. He shivered involuntarily, then sat forward in the driver's seat, squinting into the darkness beyond. A wave of weariness clutched at him and the cold that had crept into his legs now threatened to engulf the rest of his body. He glanced at his wristwatch – 2 a.m. – another ten minutes and he would be back home in the warmth of his bed.

During the afternoon the sky had cleared. By early evening the moors above Morvah shimmered from the intense heat of the sun. After the meal, Bottrell had taken his pipe and wandered up the narrow track behind the farmhouse in an attempt to clear his mind of alcohol and the haunting dreams which had tormented him. Bob had arrived home late, looking hot and weary. He therefore didn't feel inclined to quiz his friend about the details of the murder case. However, his reluctance to ask questions was not borne out of respect for the lateness of Bob's arrival or his somewhat morose frame of mind. It was rather that he simply feared the confirmation of his dreams. He had been right before about such dreams – uncannily so, and he knew that this time it would not be any different. When he had lived in London Frances had persuaded him to attend a spiritualist church with her. He had been reluctant to do so, since he was neither a Christian nor a clairvoyant. To Frances, who believed in reincarnation and used tarot cards on a regular basis, his 'gift' as she termed it, was something both unique and valuable. To Bottrell, on the other hand, it often seemed like a curse. The unwanted intruder appeared like a face at the window of his unconscious mind, bidding him to do its will.

But he was unable to deny the clarity and urgency of the dreams. On occasion, he had tried both alcohol and sleeping pills to muddy the waters. Nothing worked. The experience at the spiritualist meeting had only succeeded in angering him. In a large dilapidated hall he had sat with a community of the bereaved and disconsolate, all there to receive some crumb of comfort about those who had passed 'beyond the veil', into the realm of 'Summerland' as the jargon put it. The medium who stood before him, an unlikely, dumpy, middle-aged woman with a Birmingham accent, smelling of cheap perfume, appeared to succeed by sheer chance. How it worked he was not quite sure, but a great deal of her utterances could have applied to any of her assembled clients. Yet she held them all in her thrall. Bottrell knew that his own ability was nothing like that of the self-proclaimed medium. He could not claim to be telepathic. He was even unable to control his dreams. Instead they controlled him.

The sun was low on the horizon as he made his way up the

escarpment, past the ruined mining stack and the walls of long-deserted buildings that once played host to Cornish miners. This treeless landscape appealed to him because of its vast emptiness. In such a place he could detach himself from the world of appearances, distance himself even from his own consciousness, lose his soul in this windswept wilderness. As he climbed upwards, he recalled the story he had been told in the pub about the ghost of a man often seen here cycling at breakneck speed down the valley, his face streaming with blood. The spectre was glimpsed on the anniversary of a mining disaster when men were buried down there in the dark, cold earth. Although he described himself as a rationalist he believed in such stories. The aboriginals believed that each place in the landscape told its own story. Perhaps that was also true for him.

The chill of the approaching darkness caught at his chest. He buttoned up his jacket. Above him, he could see the outline of the great quoit, towering against the deepening sky. When he had last been in Cornwall, he had picked up a book of legends collected by an eccentric Cornishman bearing his own name. Between its pages were tales of elementals who haunted such places as this. Not the diminutive sort with gossamer wings he had read about at school, but ugly, spiteful beings called spriggans who could drive a man mad if he dared to venture into their domain. To walk in this ancient landscape, among these stones and burial mounds, it was impossible not to believe in these old tales.

He was now almost at the top and within a few yards of the rock itself, a huge oval rock that could be rocked backwards and forwards with some difficulty. He recalled the substance of his dream. What if the murdered woman had been the victim of some occult conspiracy? Here, at the edge of the land, such a possibility did not surprise him. He remembered that Zennor itself was supposed to have been the favourite haunt of the notorious black magician, Aleister Crowley. It was probably just one of those stories, but he could understand its origins in the imagination of those who lived in these remote parts. There were other stories, too, which told of witches dancing on the stones here at Halloween. Fantasy? Maybe.

He sat down on the edge of the rocking stone, reached into his jacket pocket, then lit his pipe. The familiar taste of the sweet tobacco began to soothe his spirits. Across the hillside, long fingers of shadow broke the gorse into strips. Here and there, small beacons of light from scattered farmhouses below gleamed from the encroaching darkness.

He began to think about the young woman he had seen in the café. He had not thought about a woman that way since Frances had died. He wasn't sure what it was about her that had stirred him quite that way. She didn't look like Frances. There was a strength about her that he had found appealing. He hoped that he might meet her again. A foolish thought, yet one that made him smile momentarily. He relit his pipe, which had expired some minutes ago without his even noticing it. He hadn't smiled for a long while. These days he rarely smiled.

Suddenly he felt cold. The darkness was all about him now, like the wing of a great bird drawn across the hillside. Reluctantly he made his way back down the track towards the lights of the Lean farmhouse, still smiling to himself.

The following morning Lean was up early. In the room with the gothic window, Bottrell stirred as he heard his friend banging about in the bathroom. He sat up in bed and pondered whether to share the content of his dreams with his old acquaintance. Then his indolence got the better of him and he slumped back under the duvet, staring at the ribbon of sunlight that edged its way across the bedside table. How would Lean regard him if he did divulge his visions? Would he think him crazy? Bob Lean was a man of practicalities with no apparent interest in matters psychic. It was Hazel who took note of such things as horoscopes. On one occasion, he well remembered, she had even consulted a faith healer to provide some relief for her problematical back. Bob had been downright sceptical about the matter, although, mysteriously, she had improved noticeably shortly after the treatment. No, it would be better to say nothing, as he had always done. Unless, of course, the dreams presented evidence the police did not have access to. If that possibility arose, then maybe he would offer his services. He sat up in bed, unable to resolve the question. There was something which deeply disturbed him about this case. It was no ordinary murder, no *crime passionel.* He was convinced of that. Where the conviction sprang from he had no idea. Yet he had learned over the years to trust such gut feelings. The contents of the most recent 'vision' (a term he kept strictly to himself) had confirmed that the woman had been murdered because of some kind of occult conspiracy. And the figure in the room with her also intrigued him. He sensed a power, an authority emanating from this man. He felt equally sure that if he met him in the flesh he might know him.

Down in the kitchen, Lean polished off the piece of toast and marmalade he had been eating, wiped his mouth and gave Hazel a perfunctory kiss on the cheek.

'Must love you and leave you. A long one I guess. A suspect to interview. Give you a ring on the mobile?'

Hazel nodded wearily. She was used to such exchanges.

'How's John doing? Didn't see much of him yesterday.'

'OK-ish. Though I think he's still drinking. Found an empty whisky bottle by the bed. Thought I might take him to look at the new gallery at Boscean. Help take his mind off matters.'

'Good idea. It may help. Anyway, I must be off.'

Lean took the coastal road to Pendeen. At this hour there was little traffic about, save for a few agricultural vehicles that occasionally appeared out of side turnings to test his concentration. Powell's address was some way from the crossroads on a grim-looking housing estate that appeared as if it had been put together by a Lego collector. Number 23 lay in a short terrace facing a scarred green where last night's six-pack cases and chip wrappers vied for space across the mottled sward. Three shaven-headed youths who stood abusing each other with Midlands accents blocked the approach road. Lean avoided them by driving onto the grass and was also careful to lock the door of the Hyundai before approaching the property. He pressed a disconnected door bell, then, after a long pause, knocked loudly. A slatternly-looking woman smoking a roll-up appeared behind a door chain.

'Yes?'

He showed his warrant card.

'Police. I'd like to speak to Paul Powell. Is he in?'

From the other side of the door chain, a wave of cheap perfume assailed him.

'Paul? Visitor!' The voice was a piece of glass paper, rotating inside his ear drum.

Lean waited at the door. After a few seconds, a tall, pale-faced youth appeared, dressed in a stained T-shirt and a pair of creased boxer shorts.

'Paul Powell? DI Lean. I have a few questions to ask you in connection with the death of Rebecca Wearne. I believe you were acquainted.'

Powell eyed him uneasily.

'How did you get my address?'

'Let's discuss that down at the station, shall we?'

'I'm just finishing breakfast.'

'Then I'll wait.'

The slatternly faced woman was at the door behind Paul, blowing a plume of smoke into Lean's face.

'What's up? What's he s'posed to have done?'

'Are you his mother?'

'Stepmother.'

'Tell him not to be too long.'

Lean walked back slowly to the car. The youths had now moved further up the street and were fighting each other with baseball bats. Suddenly the old name for this country came to him. 'Hard Rock Country.' It still applied.

By mid-morning the intense sunshine had given way to wreaths of dank fog. They crept in, swathing the hills around Zennor like huge rolls of cotton wool. So oppressive was the atmosphere that Bottrell gave up all attempts to light his pipe. He replaced the sodden box of matches in his jacket pocket and made his way back into the house. Inside, he found Hazel stuffing armfuls of clothes into the washing machine.

'That's it. All done now. How about checking out that new gallery in Boscean?'

Bottrell recalled the review in the arts magazine she had shown him the previous day.

'OK. I'd like that.'

She probably thinks I'm a miserable bastard, he thought. I don't know why she makes the effort. She'll probably be glad to see me leave. And she knows about the drinking problem. That empty bottle by the bedside cabinet. Not there this morning. There's a supermarket in St Just. Perhaps I can refuel from there.

'How about lunch at that café in St Just?' he suggested. 'On me, of course.'

'Sounds great.'

Hazel smiled at him. She was standing with her back to the sunlight and her hair was shining. He noticed that it was a deep, lustrous shade. He thought how long it had been since he had been with a woman and the thought brought him up sharply.

The coast road was almost terrifying in its other-worldliness. The sea and the cliffs were quite invisible and all that could be seen were occasional glimpses of stone walls and the glaring headlights of an oncoming car. Progress was painfully slow. Fog had always had the effect of inducing a kind of hypnotic trance in Bottrell. As he listened to the slow beat of the windscreen wipers, he found himself slipping into a profound reverie. He was halfway through a fantasy about the girl in the café leaning over him at the table when he was suddenly aware that the car was veering to the left, down a narrow lane which dipped steeply into an ancient valley lined with beech and oak.

'This is Boscean,' Hazel explained.

Boscean. The name was familiar to him. There was a story about it, he was sure. Something about a man from Sancreed who lost his way on midsummer's eve and ended up in a ruined chapel where he was tormented by a goat-like figure. In the early morning his friends found his lacerated body at the foot of some rocks at Beacon Hill, some miles off. A strange, haunted landscape, thought Bottrell, winding down the car window and peering out at the twisted hawthorns and ancient oaks. Not a place he could safely live in for very long.

Boscean turned out to be a tiny hamlet. No post office. Not even a church. A cluster of farm buildings and a smell of fresh manure. At the end of a lane, Hazel stopped the car and they walked the 200 yards to the converted Methodist chapel still bearing the inscription 'Bible Christian' on its lintel. As Hazel pushed open the door, a bell rang from inside. Just like the opening scene in Dracula, Bottrell mused.

Inside, there was a smell compounded of old damp timbers and beeswax. The gallery had been sympathetically restored and whoever now owned it had gone to some trouble to preserve some of the original features. A number of church candles had been placed in niches beneath the tall, pointed windows. On an improvised altar in the middle of the gallery an oil burner threw out the sweet smell of lavender. But it was not these trappings which caught Bottrell's attention.

Around the perimeter of the gallery hung several large oil paintings. There was a clear unity of themes among them. The first showed a clearing in an ancient forest. In the foreground the figures of a naked man and woman lay stretched out beside a rock. Observing them from a gap in the trees stood a Pan-like figure with cloven hoofs. The implication in the painting was clear: that the couple had somehow been entranced by the place. Bottrell thought that the painting held for him a strange fascination. It was like a dream.

'Would you care for a catalogue?' A tall young woman with hennaed hair stood holding out a leaflet headed: 'Asmodeus Gallery. Fine Art & Sculpture.' She had a strong smell of patchouli oil about her which he found faintly arousing.

'Am I speaking to the artist?'

'One of them. I'm Carmilla. Peter is the other artist. My partner. He's the sculptor.'

He gave the sculptures a cursory glance. Most of them were large, crude affairs, carved from what appeared to be bog oak. To his untrained eye they all seemed strangely masculine.

'Feel free to look around.'

Bottrell observed Carmilla intently. There was something rather fey about her. She wore the uniform of the traveller: nose jewellery, tie-dyed T-shirt, silk skirt, heavy boots. But it wasn't that which drew his attention. There was something almost predatory about her movements, he thought. She was like some kind of perfumed spider, moving inexorably along her web as she strode about the gallery. It was then that he noticed the little silver pentagram attached to her T-shirt.

'So tell me about this painting.'

He was aware that she had been staring oddly at him.

'It's based on a medieval folk tale.'

'An allegorical painting?'

She nodded.

'Kind of. In the story a couple enter an ancient wildwood. The wood has a guardian – a satyr. When they try to leave, they can never find their way out. Way out is down through the earth – the underworld. Actually, the wood is based on a copse near here – close to the village.'

But he had not heard the explanation. He was staring intently at the pentagram on the girl's shirt. What interested him was that it was inverted.

Paul Powell sat in interrogation room number 2. He was still wearing the stained green T-shirt, although the boxer shorts had been concealed by an equally grubby pair of faded denims. Since he had not shaved or washed for two days, he looked decidedly rough. His hair, long and matted, hung limply to his shoulders. His hands cradled a polystyrene cup containing the standard revolting machine coffee known affectionately by members of the force at Police HQ as 'gnat's piss'.

Lean entered with Robertson and sat down opposite him. He nodded to the uniformed PC by the door, then switched on the machine. After a few words of introduction to the audiotape, Lean asked:

'How well did you know Rebecca Wearne, Paul?'

'I was her boyfriend a while back.'

'Not recently then?'

'No, we had a disagreement.'

'When was that, Paul?'

'Dunno. 'Bout a month ago, I s'pose. You haven't got a fag I could have, I s'pose?'

Robertson offered him one.

'So what happened then – about the disagreement?'

'I told you. We fell out.'

'How exactly? Did you hit her?'

'I got pissed off with her. No, I never hit her.'

'And what – you left her? She left you? Which?'

'I left her. She wanted too much of her own way. Way too much.'

'But you continued to run the shop with her? Despite the disagreement.'

'The shop was a business arrangement. I put up half the money as an investment. Worked bloody hard for it. Wasn't going to pull out just because.... It was necessity.'

'Can you account for your movements on the evening of Wednesday July 27th?'

Powell drew hard on his cigarette, then plumed the smoke towards the ceiling. 'I don't exactly remember. Think I went shopping at Tesco's. Then came back and had a couple of drinks. That was it.'

'There's no one who can verify that account, is there? Your mother, for example?'

'Stepmother?'

'OK. Stepmother. I'm asking if you can prove your whereabouts?'

'Look, are you going to charge me, or just piss me about? Because if you are, I want a solicitor.'

Lean stood up, spoke into the tape recorder, then turned it off.

'OK. Listen, Paul. Listen carefully. Your car was spotted on the evening of July 27th, close to the rocks where we discovered Rebecca's body. Give me one good reason why you were in the vicinity that evening. Because if you can't, you're going to need a solicitor.

While Robertson continued with the interrogation, Lean, accompanied by a WPC, took the A30 to Hayle, then followed the coast road via Zennor to Pendeen. The early fog had lifted and a brilliant blue sky now lightened the greyness of the estate houses. This time Lean had no problem parking the car. The ravaged green playing space was no longer occupied by the crop-headed youths. The only person in view was an ancient woman carrying two overfilled carrier bags to her front door.

'Give you a hand with those, love?'

The old woman eyed him suspiciously.

'I'm all right, thanks.'

Lean shrugged his shoulders. The WPC smiled, then looked away, obviously amused by the uncharacteristic display of chivalry.

'Powell's house is Number 23,' he said, curtly. Don't bother with the bell. It doesn't work.'

WPC Blaise, who had grown accustomed to Lean's abrupt manner, continued smiling to herself and knocked loudly on the paint-peeled door. There was a long pause before Powell's stepmother appeared behind the chain, eyeing her suspiciously, clad in a thin nylon negligée.

'What do you want?'

'Mrs Powell?'

'Clarke. My name's Clarke. And this isn't a good moment.'

Behind the bedraggled figure of Mrs Clarke a large, paunchy middle-aged man wearing only a bath towel, called out.

'Who is it, Fran?'

Lean stepped forward.

'Sorry if it isn't convenient, Mrs Clarke, but I have a warrant to search these premises.'

The small bedroom on the first floor which belonged to Paul was cluttered to the brim with an assortment of books, videotapes and magazines. Lean knelt by the bookcase and rummaged through the collection. Several of the magazines were stapled and amateurishly produced, bearing titles like 'SABS' and 'Direct Action News'. A good proportion of the books were of an occult nature and there were heavier, academic tomes like Thompson's 'Making of the English Working Class'. Nothing ordinary or predictable about this young man's tastes, Lean mused.

'No sign of any electric flex, sir', commented WPC Blaise, who was examining the contents of a small gloss-painted dressing table.

'I wouldn't expect to find it here,' Lean answered. He had glimpsed a pile of magazines hidden inside a manilla folder. He pulled out the first copy which bore the title: 'S & M'. The front cover depicted a young woman swathed in rubber who had been handcuffed and was spread-eagled face downwards on a bed. Towering over her was a well-oiled muscled youth. He was naked except for a leather thong, and in his left hand was a whip. Lean flicked through the pages of the magazine and caught sight of further scenes of degradation.

'Take a look at these.' WPC Blaise did not even blanch at the material, having seen it all before.

'Our Mr Powell is a young man with very diverse tastes, it would appear,' he observed.

'More perverse than diverse. Do you think he killed her, sir?'

Lean stared at the magazine and pondered Powell's relationship with Rebecca. If they had both gone in for this sort of thing, might he just have killed her by accident, then dumped the body in a panic?

'He might have done. Put these in a bag, will you?'

As he stood up, the bedroom door opened behind him. A sullen-faced Mrs Clarke stood facing him with her arms folded. Her negligée had been discarded in favour of a tight, low-cut T-shirt and her unfettered, ample breasts seemed only to augment her aggressive stance.

'How long are you going to be? I've got a doctor's appointment at 2.30.'

Lean stared at the tattooed fish on her neck.

'Mrs Clarke, I don't know if you appreciate the gravity of the situation, but I'm conducting a murder case in which your son may be implicated. I also have questions I'd like to ask you. Now we can attend to that later if you have a medical appointment. Meanwhile, I have a job to do. I'll let myself out when I've finished.'

Mrs Clarke unfolded her arms, taken aback by the bluntness of the retort. Then she turned, muttered something abusive and stomped her way back downstairs. WPC Blaise, who had found this exchange somewhat amusing, feigned interest in the bondage magazine, then slid it back into the folder.

'Is there anything else you want me to do, sir?'

'Oh I'm sure there will be, WPC Blaise.'

Bottrell had been relieved when finally they left the gallery. He had found the presence of the young woman strangely unnerving. Her paintings were odd, claustrophobic, cloying affairs. But that wasn't entirely it. He had the distinct conviction that the pale-faced woman not only had known Rebecca Wearne but that there was some link between her and her death. It was entirely irrational, but he also knew that such hunches had proved valuable in the past.

He turned to Hazel.

'I'm hungry.'

'OK. Let's do lunch.'

'And I'd like to look at that occult bookshop – if it's open.'

He felt a sudden conviction that the shop would provide one more link in the chain that as yet, he could only dimly perceive. He allowed himself a brief smile. As Holmes would say: 'One cannot theorize without data.' And data was what he needed most of all now.

Chapter Three

It had been a dark night when they set out. He remembered how reluctant he had been to go in the first place, yet because he hadn't wished to disappoint Frances, he had at last given way. It had been his choice to drive. He invariably drove, partly because of Frances' short-sightedness and partly because driving acted as a kind of therapy for him. On that fateful day, he had brought the Turner case to its inevitable conclusion. He had been glad to see the back of the business. Turner was a paedophile who, for ten years, had operated a child pornography business on the internet from his vicarage in Walthamstow. It had been an unsavoury case and had tested Bottrell's patience to the limit. So the two-hour drive into the countryside provided him with a welcome opportunity to relax.

Because Frances had not seen her parents for a while, she had been animated during the meal. Her father, who was something of a raconteur, had regaled John with stories about his subversive activities on Guernsey during the war. The old man, although physically disabled, had lost none of his sharp wit. However, by 11.30, John had begun to feel a wave of weariness descend upon him. At midnight they had begun the long journey home.

In retrospect, he knew it had been a terrible error of judgement. They could have stayed over and driven back the next morning. Frances' parents wouldn't have minded. Yet because he was stubborn, because he always had to take control of the situation – because of all this, he had, in effect, killed his wife. Despite all their friends' protestations to the contrary, he told himself he was directly responsible for what had happened to Frances.

During the first part of the journey they had chatted spasmodically. Then Frances had fallen asleep. He turned the car cassette deck on and listened to an old Rolling Stones tape. It was then that he began to give way to waves of weariness that had been lurking within him all evening. Once he had left the motorway, he had slipped into a network of small roads and was plunged into darkness. Although he remembered the route vaguely, he was unsure of his precise bearings, but he had no desire to waken Frances, who was now sleeping soundly beside him, her head lolling on his shoulder.

As the night wore on, he became increasingly confused and at last pulled up in a lay-by where he studied the road map by the light of a small torch. He knew that he was somewhere near the Kent border. He looked up. Ahead of him he could see the curve of the Weald and beyond it lay the M20. He followed the minor road until at last he came to a crossroads with a pub on the corner, then found himself entering the slip road for the motorway. The lights dazzled him, the illuminated signs flashing past in quick succession. Now that he was back on the main arterial route he began to relax and turned up the volume on the tape deck.

Then he lost time. There were moments when he wished that time might be reinstated.If only to salvage his tortured conscience. It was as if some unruly hand had turned a switch in his brain and sent him straight to hell. All he remembered was the sudden nightmare sensation of the car leaving the motorway and veering down the bank to the accompaniment of blaring horns and the helpless sensation of being unable to control the wheel. Then the concrete pillar loomed from the darkness and he was aware of the steering wheel hitting his chest and his wife's body hurtling through the windscreen.

There followed a prolonged silence in which the darkness of the ditch and the taste of his own blood was overwhelming. He could not move. He was trapped behind the wheel. He was sure that the pain in his chest indicated a broken rib. But that was not the worst of it. The worst thing was seeing the deep arterial blood curling down Frances' legs as she twitched and moaned through her last moments. He could not reach her. His arms were trapped. He could only cry out to her in the icy darkness and hope that she could hear him.

After some while he lapsed into unconsciousness and was woken only by the sound of the emergency services' vehicles' sirens. But by that time Frances was dead.

The terrible guilt he had experienced that night in the wrecked Mercedes had never left him. Sleeping or waking, it had followed him like a shadow, always lurking just beyond reach, reminding him of his failings. No amount of counselling or psychotherapy could remove it. He had sought comfort in booze, but when he awoke from its temporary anaesthesia, the shadow was still there, pointing the finger at him. At last, that dark shadow spread its inky blackness into his working life. He began to lose concentration, then his patience, and ultimately his reason. It was then that his colleagues, and especially his superiors in the Met, began to sit up and take notice.

Then had come the fateful day. Sitting in a surveillance car in Rotherhithe, he had allowed himself to fall into a deep slumber as his colleague grappled with three hoodlums and lost the fight. The enquiry that followed found him guilty of gross negligence. It had been the final straw. He had betrayed not only his wife but also a trusted friend and colleague. After that, he had sought oblivion.

It was Bob and Hazel who had sought him out and encouraged him to dry out. They had shown forbearance and patience. They had offered him a chance to detach himself from his sorrow and it had been their idea for him to return to a place where once he had been happy and contented. So he had begun the long journey from Paddington to Penzance, unsure of what his future held for him, uncertain even of who he was anymore.

With this state of confusion and blank despair had come the dreams. Stronger than before, more real than ever. He had had dreams before this, but never in such vivid detail.

All this he recalled between the moment that Hazel pulled in at St Just square and the moment he got out of the car and stared across at the shop with its tarot decks and figurines, bedded on green velvet.

Extract from Rebecca Wearne's Diary

12th January 1999

Have been going through some of Jane's correspondence and diaries from 1997. Found this:

> *'How hast thou fallen from Heaven, Helel's Son, Shaker. Thou didst say in thy heart, I will ascend to heaven, above the circumpolar stars I will raise my throne, and I will dwell on the Mount of Council in the back of the north; I will mount on the back of a cloud. I will be like unto Elyon.'*

Don't think she wrote it herself. Am convinced it's a quote from some ancient text. I have a feeling that if I could only place it into context, it would give me some clue as to her involvement with 'The Wise One'. Spoke to her friend, Susan, last Tuesday. She was a member of the 'moot' but she didn't seem to know anything about 'The Wise One'. I wasn't sure if she was telling me the truth.

24th January 1999

Very tired at present. Heavy week at work. No further progress with Jane's whereabouts. It's all quite depressing, really. Have been reading through her most recent diary. Have found the source of the quote – although the text is not quite the same. It had been rolling round the back of my tortured brain for weeks until it finally clicked. Showed the text to Peter, our book shop manager (who's an orthodox Jew). Lucky me... He told me it's a different form of a passage from Isaiah (14.12–14):

> *'How are thou fallen from Heaven, O Lucifer, son of the*

morning. For thou hast said in thine heart, I will ascend to heaven, I will exalt my throne above the stars of God. I will also sit upon the mount of the congregation, in the sides of the north: I will ascend above the heights of the clouds, I will be like the most High.'

Peter reckons the version in Jane's diary is from a seventh-century pagan text. How on earth did she come by this? There's much more I need to know.

10th February 1999

Have discovered something interesting. It may be a lead. Peter was telling me about the bookshop on the corner of Wallace Street, which used to be an alternative bookshop called Utopia, at the time Anne worked here. Then I remembered that among Anne's book collection were two volumes: *Magic in Theory & Practice* and *Diary of a Drug Fiend*, by Aleister Crowley. On the flyleaf of both was an address label bearing the name 'Utopia'. According to Peter, the owner of the Utopia bookshop was the leader of an occult group called The Brethren of The Morning Star. Peter didn't know much about the group but he said they conducted their meetings in a room above the bookshop. There were around twenty members – some ex-wiccans, mainly men. The group lasted for around a year before it folded. I am convinced that Anne was linked with this group.

1st March 1999

(News cutting pasted from the *Western Morning News*, pasted into diary, dated 2nd November 1997).

CHRISTIAN PROTEST AT 'BLACK MAGIC' SHOP.
An occult bookshop in Exeter has been the target of a protest by local Christians. The Utopia bookshop in Wallace Street was yesterday picketed by a group of about 30 people who sang hymns and leafleted passers by. The Utopia bookshop, which was opened about six months ago, was last week the subject of an attack by a local Methodist minister, Mr Brian Jackson. 'The shop is a recruiting ground for Satanists,' claimed Mr Jackson. 'We have had several cases of young people purchasing Ouija boards from this shop. At least three of them have since had very disturbing experiences through dabbling with the occult. Such experimentation is extremely dangerous.'

Local Baptist minister Robert Dunbarton also expressed his concern about the bookshop. 'No one objects to people following their own religious beliefs,' he claimed. 'However, this shop is a front for very sinister activities. I have spoken to other leaders of local Christian groups. We are determined that this shop should not stay open.'

The owner of Utopia, Mr Keith Slade, refused to comment on the protest or the accusations levelled against him. A police spokesman commented that they were not aware of a problem regarding the bookshop. The shop sells a number of magical artifacts, including tarot cards, incense, crystals and a wide selection of books on the occult. Mr Slade said that he intended to continue trading, despite the protest.

7th March 1999

Checked the electoral registers at the county reference library. Found a Keith Slade living at No. 2 Wallace Street in 1997. No other persons at this address. Gone by 1998. Anne was also gone in the spring of that year. Is this a coincidence?

14th March 1999

Found Robert Dunbarton, the Baptist minister, at last. He recalled Slade quite clearly and was able to give me an accurate description of him. He also remembered Anne after I had described her to him. He recalled her working in the shop on the three occasions he had visited the place. He showed me a leaflet he had picked up from the shop that he believed demonstrated that Slade was recruiting for his 'Satanist' group. He's allowed me to take a copy of the leaflet. It makes for interesting reading.

Slotting the diary pages, news cutting and leaflet into the envelope, he sealed it, then placed it in a small escritoire by his bedside, which he locked. For several minutes he sat, staring into his glass of whisky. He stood up, drained it, then moved to the window. Outside the night was charcoal black. Through the trees a milky moon shone behind rain-laden clouds. The moon was nearly in her full aspect now. It would then be time. In the eastern sky, Shalem, the evening star, shone for a moment, then was obscured behind a bank of cloud. He turned from the window, closed the curtains, then extinguished the bedside lamp.

The café had been crowded. Most of the customers were clearly tourists. Many of them carried back-packs and traces of the coastal footpath mud on their recently acquired and polished boots. They huddled around the tables, exchanging stories, their faces ruddy from the recent westerlies which had assailed them on the moors and cliffs.

Bottrell had been glad to leave behind the bonhomie atmosphere and smell of hand-rolled tobacco. He felt introspective. He always became introspective when he thought of Frances. Somehow the death of the young woman on the cliff had brought back only too keenly the memory of that fateful evening. He knew from the way his psyche worked that more was to follow. It was like having a clock ticking away inside his head. Sooner or later, the hour hand would hit the alarm and he would see something or dream something that one or two days later he would be able to verify through independent means. That was the way it always worked.

Hazel had sensed his impatience.

'You wanted to visit the shop across the way?' she said, breaking his reverie.

'Yes, why not? Pick up a spell book or two. Thought I might try necromancy for a change,' he joked.

'OK. Look, I've got some books I need to return to the library. See you back at the car for lunch? Twenty minutes?'

He nodded.

Outside, brilliant shafts of sunlight had lit up the pools of rainwater which scarred the tarred surface of the road, so that they were almost blinded as they made their way across the square.

He peered through the window of 'The Moon Stallion.' His trained eye noted that the athame had disappeared, to be replaced by a small, rather ugly doll, bearing the label 'Goddess Figure.' Underneath this title, the caption read: 'Handmade terracotta goddess figure. Hand cast from Cornish clay. Glazed, using non-toxic materials. This original figure may be used for meditation or as a good luck charm.'

Bottrell smiled at the new age sentiments, then pushed open the shop door. From inside came a heavy odour of cheap incense which he traced to a small fertility figure fashioned into a burner. To his left stood a tall, aquiline-faced man with sleek black hair, pulled back into a pony-tail. It was clear that his entry into the shop had interrupted an intense conversation with the blonde-haired woman Bottrell now recalled from the café.

The pony-tailed man muttered something incomprehensible, then turned and left, leaving a trail of expensive aftershave behind him. Bottrell smiled disarmingly, then glanced around at the contents of the shop. There was a fairly extensive collection of modern books on paganism and a second-hand section that included a history of witchcraft and several books by Aleister Crowley.

A notice board to his left bearing several business cards, immediately attracted his attention. A wide variety of practitioners ranging from Reiki healers to homeopaths was represented. In the middle of the notice board, an A5 sheet bearing the legend 'Pagan Moot' drew his interest, giving the date and pub location of the group's meetings along with the words: 'All Are Welcome'. He took a small notebook from his coat pocket and made a note of it. He scanned the leaflets, then he bent down and picked up a small glossy brochure headed 'The Key To Thelema'. Bottrell looked up and smiled. Close up the blonde-haired woman was even more attractive than he had first imagined. Her skin colour was sallow. Her eyes dark and penetrating. They held his gaze for what seemed a long few seconds.

'Hello, are you new to the area?'

'On holiday actually.'

As he spoke, he could see Hazel smiling at him through the window of the shop. He raised a hand in recognition.

'Looking for a particular practitioner?' She gestured at the notice board.

'I was wondering about this,' he observed, pointing to the pagan moot notice.

'There's a meeting tomorrow if you'd like to attend. At the Old Buttery. We're very friendly. By the way, I'm Anne.'

'Pleased to meet you, Anne.'

She stretched out a long sinewy arm. Bottrell grasped it. The grip was firm, the flesh comfortingly warm to the touch.

'And you are...?'

'John. John Bottrell.'

'Pleased to meet you, John.'

By now Hazel had entered the shop and was standing behind him, pretending to absorb herself in some Celtic jewellery.

'Anyway, I must ... we must ... go.' He ended lamely, aware of Hazel's wry smile in the mirror opposite.

'I think I'll take these,' added Hazel, presenting her with a pair of silver earrings. He shifted uneasily as the transaction was completed.

After lunch had been concluded, they left the café and made their way across the car park.

'Get everything?'

Hazel nodded.

'You seemed to be hitting it off rather well, I thought.'

'Just following up something.'

She gazed at him quizzically.

'And that something is...?'

'Something to do with the girl on the cliff. I have a hunch. That's all.'

'I'm not sure I see the connection.'

'No, nor do I. Not yet,' he murmured.

He lapsed into silence as the car wove its way from the square, down a narrow side-road, past the imposing façade of the town's enormous Methodist chapel. To Bottrell's discerning eye, the streets seemed unusually busy. Large groups of young people, wearing the customary baseball caps, trainers and jeans, appeared to be moving towards the perimeter of the town, so that after some while Hazel was forced to move the car into the centre of the road in order to avoid them.

'What's up?' he quizzed.

'I'm not sure. Some sort of demonstration I think.'

As they turned into the main coastal road they came to an abrupt halt behind a police van containing several bored looking officers wearing flak jackets. Beyond, Bottrell glimpsed someone who he guessed was a police inspector, engaged in an earnest conversation with a press photographer. As the road snaked round to the left, he could also make out a collection of approximately 60 protesters, who had formed a seated circle around a figure dressed incongruously as a badger.

Bottrell opened the passenger door to the now stationary car and peered over the roof.

'What's happening?' asked Hazel.

'There's a man dressed as a badger chained to a lamp post,' Bottrell replied. 'And a PC with bolt cutters, doing his damnedest to free him.'

Hazel turned off the ignition and joined him at the vantage point.

The sun broke from behind a solitary cloud and had now thrown the protester into sharp relief. There was a metallic snap as the chain broke, coupled with a howl of derision from the erstwhile peaceful crowd of sitters. As if on a pre-arranged signal they now rose and began a low, sustained chant as they circled the solitary PC.

Bottrell, who had given way to an overwhelming curiosity, was now pushing his way through the crowd with swift strides. Ahead, he could see that the crowd were unremitting in their desire to make a point and the PC was looking round edgily. He watched as the press photographer, who had now managed to scale the wall to the adjoining park, began to capture the moment.

What followed seemed to be over in a second, almost as if the whole incident had been executed on film.

The figure in the badger suit raised its arms and, flashing the chain above its head, charged at the police officer. The crowd surged from behind him and the officer slipped from view like a leaf enveloped in a river torrent. Bottrell was now in the thick of the mêlée. Using his elbows to make headway, he forced his way to a point where he could glimpse the legs and arms of the fallen officer.

Suddenly the circle around him began to break. Just beyond the company of surging protesters he could make out the blue uniforms of the uniformed police and the occasional flash of a baton.

He was now surrounded by what seemed like a sea of human suffering. Faces came and went, some bewildered, others puce with anger. A man's hand protruded between two unconnected arms and grabbed at his throat but he immediately disengaged the attack with his free arm. He was down on the ground now, bent over the injured officer in an attitude resembling the Madonna and child, cradling his blood-spattered head. Behind him he could hear the sharp imperatives of the commanding officer. Slowly the scuffling and abuse began to subside. Feeling a hand on his back, he turned and found himself staring at Bob Lean's craggy features.

'What on earth are you doing here?'

'Helping out, it seems.'

'I think I can manage.'

In the distance Bottrell could hear the wail of the approaching ambulance. The fallen man groaned and attempted to raise himself from the ground, his mouth twisted in pain.

'Easy, easy....'

Bottrell stood up, allowing his friend to take charge. All around him small groups of protesters were being hustled into lines, awaiting their imminent arrest. Behind him, the road was now clear and he was aware of Hazel's anxious face, peering at him. Disappointed at Lean's intervention, he made his way back to the car, sat down, then lit his pipe to calm his nerves. He sat for some while next to Hazel as she plied him with questions. Yes, everything was now under control, he assured her. No serious injuries. No, Bob was fine. The taste of the aromatic tobacco was sweet upon his lips. As Hazel put the car into first gear, he glanced about him. At the far end of the street he saw the girl from the bookshop striding towards them, her coat flapping in the wind. It was an athletic, purposeful stride. For some strange reason she fascinated him. Her head thrown back, she resembled a figure he had once seen in a Burne-Jones painting. There was something rather other-worldly about her, he decided. He thought he would like to see her again.

Bottrell stood before the open window. Already the sun had reached the edge of the Penwith hills, casting them into a black brood of crouched figures. How animate they seemed against the orange sky. How unwilling to be subdued by the odd farm building that sat uncomfortably on their surface. The notion so troubled him that he closed the curtains, switched on the bedside lamp and reached for the small leaflet he had picked up in the occult bookshop.

'The Key To Thelema,' he read: 'The Ancient Teachings Of The Guardian Spirits, as transcribed by Simon Matthias, Minister of the Great Lodge.'

He turned the page. Inside, the text continued:

> All the great religions of the world share one truth: that behind the world of the visible, the world of illusion, lies the world of the unseen. From time immemorial the guiding spirits of this unseen world have attempted to counsel frail humanity. Yet such is our ignorance, we have remained blind to their Message.
>
> Down through the centuries, the Great Message from this invisible world has been communicated through many prophets: Moses, Jesus, Mohammed. But since the advent of the Age of Aquarius, new prophets have arisen.

He paused, reached for the bottle of malt from inside the bedside table and poured himself a large tumbler full of the golden liquid. For some moments he sat staring at the glass before putting it to his lips and downing it in one, rapacious go. Then he lay back on the pillows and breathed a sigh. It was a sigh of utter weariness, not physical weariness but a deep weariness of the soul. He recalled the incident in the town square, the mad jostling, pushing and screaming that was often the keynote of humanity. The words on the page in front of him seemed to Bottrell to fit that order of things, that intense striving to prove a point, to be right beyond doubt, to possess the truth at whatever cost to the individual or maybe the entire human race. Slowly the paper slid from his grasp and fluttered to the floor. His eyelids drooped.

In his dream the room was dark. The man who stood in the centre of the darkened room was who he expected to see: the tall, thin-faced man with the pony-tail from the bookshop. He was dressed in a kind of long kaftan and wore an amber necklace around his neck. He could smell the cloying stench of musk in the room, although in the dream it was stronger than before.

Bottrell knew that although he was present in the dream, pony-tail man could not perceive his presence. It was as if he were a ghost, an interloper from another time. Thus, when pony-tail man turned to face him, he looked through him with eyes as cold as steel. The feeling of those eyes made him catch his breath, drove a snake of fear through him, so that he began to shake involuntarily. Then he gasped as pony-tail man walked straight through him.

He turned. At the far end of the darkened room a door had opened. The door was old and scratched, he recalled, as if a dog had been shut in here and could not get out. Through the door walked a young woman, dressed in white. He had expected it to be the woman he had seen in the previous dream. But it was not her. It was the woman from the bookshop. Yet there was something different about her. There was a strange luminosity in her eyes. Her face seemed suffused, as if she burned with an inner radiance. Pony-tail smiled and beckoned to her. Then the door closed, shutting out the light once more.

He awoke to the sound of rain hammering against the window

pane. Whilst he had slept a wind had arisen, blowing the curtains into the room where their sodden hems had knocked over the half-empty bottle of malt. He swore under his breath, righted the bottle, then reached for a box of tissues and began mopping up the amber liquid.

As quickly as the rain had arisen, so it ceased. He pulled back the curtains and stared out into the night. Lighting his pipe, he drew his chair up to the window and allowed the cold air to sculpt his face. The torpor of his dream began to slip away. Slowly the memory of pony-tail man began to fade. The rich smell of the aromatic tobacco curled out into the night, comforting him. Somewhere, out there, behind closed doors, there was a darkened room where the man with a pony-tail stood like some human arachnid, beckoning. First one victim, then another. He hoped he was wrong. He hoped it was nothing but a fantasy, a waking dream of no consequence. But what if the dream were true? He did not understand much at present, but he knew that the leaflet had some connection with the woman's body on the cliff path.

Then there was that word: Thelema. What was that? He watched as two distant car headlights burned yellow against the darkness of the hill beyond the cottage. Where had he come across that word before? Holmes would have called this a three pipe problem. He rummaged in his tobacco pouch. Shame. He had only enough tobacco for two pipes at the very most. Thelema. A distant memory began to surface. A book he had read years ago, when he was an undergraduate at Oxford. A French novel. He couldn't recall the name of it. But he remembered the author's name. Rabelais. Yes, that was it. Thelema was the name of his abbey. A place of licentiousness where the dictum of 'Do as you like!' held sway. And where else had he come across it? The image of Aleister Crowley, the self-styled magician floated into his mind. 'Do What Thou Wilt....' Wasn't that also his dictum? And didn't he have some sort of abbey on an island in the Mediterranean where he practised his bizarre sexual rites? Bottrell recalled reading about it.

His pipe was now extinguished. So deep had his reverie been that he had allowed it to peter out. He drew the flame of his lighter across the bowl of the pipe and it sprang into life once more.

What was the connection between pony-tail and the girl in the shop? Was there one? He wasn't sure. He wasn't sure of anything. He was possessed by an unnerving presentiment that what he had seen in the dream was a sort of prefiguring of events. That troubled him. By the time he heard the Zennor church clock strike twelve he found he had smoked through another bowlful of tobacco. His last.

When finally he shut the window and pulled the duvet over his weary body he found he was unable to extinguish the memory of the woman in white from his mind. Moreover, he could smell her perfume. As clearly as if she were here with him in the room. As clearly as if she lay sleeping beside him.

Anne.

The girl with the purposeful stride.

But what was her purpose in his dreams?

Sleep consumed him.

Chapter Four

The morning came to consciousness with the smell of the spilt whisky like some heady perfume in the room. He stirred, aware of voices from below. His head pounded like a steam hammer. He groaned, appalled by his own recklessness. The room was now icy cold and beyond the curtains, a grey sky threatened imminent rain.

Quickly, he dragged himself from under the duvet and changed into his clothes. From the bedside cabinet he drew out a packet of paracetamol tablets, poured a glass of water from the wash-basin tap and attempted to redress the effects of last night's debauch. The water tasted strangely brackish, but on the other hand that might have been a reflection on the state of his digestive system.

Thelema. The word slid back into his mind. A place of licentiousness. There was the girl from the bookshop again, stalking him through the veil of sleep. What was it about her? He had been attracted to other women since Frances' death but predictably, they much resembled her. Anne was different.

When he reached the kitchen, he found Lean devouring a hurried piece of toast whilst struggling into his jacket.

'Heavy night?'

Hazel frowned at her husband's insensitivity.

'You could say. Any progress on the murder case?'

Lean shrugged his shoulders.

'We have a suspect in custody. The boyfriend. Though we don't have any real evidence – as yet. He's just been rearrested.'

'Oh yes?'

'Remember the guy in the badger suit?'

'How can I forget him?'

Hazel smiled.

'The same. Animal rights protester. We have a suspicion he's been springing traps in the area. Possibly what he was doing the night of the murder. Though of course, he can't prove it ... there were no witnesses.'

'Do you think he did it?'

'Can't say. Hazel tells me you have some thoughts on the subject.'

'Just idle speculation I'm afraid.'

'Well let me know if you get anywhere with it. I'd appreciate your input.'

'Sure. But without a clear motive....'

Lean nodded.

'That's our problem.'

Kissing his wife goodbye, he picked up his car keys and made his way out into the hall.

Hazel offered to replenish Bottrell's mug but he demurred. She sat opposite him and finished her tea.

'You have an idea , don't you John?'

'I think there's something odd about this one. That's all. I really don't know much more. That bookshop in St Just?'

'The Moon Stallion?'

'It had an odd feeling, I thought.'

'Some strange characters get in there,' she confirmed. 'You think there may be a connection with the murdered girl?'

'I'm not sure.'

He finished his coffee and lapsed into silence.

After breakfast was concluded, he donned his waterproof coat and, pulling up the collar, made his way out into the garden. A strong, damp smell of earth and freshly cut lawn trimmings assailed him. He reached into his pocket for his pipe, then realized in some despair that he had completely run out of tobacco. He swore under his breath and then examined the sky above him. Dun-coloured clouds hung there, as Holmes's old friend Doctor Watson might have described them. He might risk it and take the footpath across the fields by the old quoit to the village shop. With any luck they might stock an aromatic tobacco to his liking.

At the end of the garden he passed through a gate and found himself in a narrow lane where high walls encompassed him on both sides. He was fairly sure the footpath petered out on to the moors. From there he could cut across the side of Zennor Quoit and drop down to the village shop.

The strangeness of the land pressed upon him as he walked with quickened pace. He was aware of the ever-changing sky and the promise of rain. This was not a place that welcomed human kind. Stranger in a stranger land. That described him perfectly. Was that why he was here? To discover the true meaning of his isolation?

He was now at the end of the footpath and on the border of the moorland. To his left lay the towering rock stack of Zennor Quoit, the summit swathed in a dense mist. Following his instincts, he climbed upwards, moving from rock to rock, their surfaces glistening and dark like the backs of primeval reptiles. His headache had cleared with the exertion and he was possessed of an extreme lucidity for which he could not account. As he climbed, he found himself breathing in great lungfuls of air. Somehow up here he no longer felt alone. Surrounded by these colossal, mute rock formations, things seemed much clearer. He knew that his alcoholism was a desperate attempt to anaesthetise himself, to dull the passing of time. But did he have the ability to move on, put the past to rest?

It was as he turned to face the valley below that he saw them: two silhouettes, circling each other inside the Quoit. He stopped and drew back so as to remain invisible. He knew one of them immediately he set eyes on him: the other he was not sure of. It might have been a woman. But the taller figure of the two was certainly pony-tail man. Of that, he could be sure. He was holding some kind of stick and waving it in the air as he moved, circular fashion from rock to rock. The other figure followed him. The dense fog muffled their sounds, yet even at this distance Bottrell could hear that they were chanting.

At last the sounds ceased. When he moved from behind the rock, they had both gone, almost as if they were nothing more than wraiths.

Mrs Clarke had just reached the point of consummation when there was a loud banging on her front door. At first she thought she would ignore the summons and give way to the continued thrusts of her large lover whose dimpled stomach now threatened to compress her diaphragm. However, since she was short of breath and needed a cigarette rather badly, she thought better of it, made her excuses, and reached for her dressing gown, leaving her portly consort to subside on the bed in a veritable bath of sweat.

Despite her repeated shouting, the banging did not cease until she had opened the door to discover a uniformed policeman accompanied by Lean and a somewhat weary looking DC Robertson.

'Mrs Clarke?'

'What the f— do you want this time? Do you realize what the f—ing time is?'

'Now then, Mrs Clarke, no need to get upset. We need to look in your garage. If you don't mind.'

'Why don't you f— off?'

'Need any help, Trace?' The sweating lover had appeared in the hallway behind her in a pair of creased pyjamas, looking dishevelled and decidedly sheepish.

'No I f—ing don't. I'll sort this out.'

'The garage if you please. We need access. We have a warrant.'

Dumbfounded by the sight of the warrant Mrs Clarke relented and led the way through the hall where a side door admitted them to the garage.

'Is there a light switch?'

'Here.'

A fitful glare from a single light bulb illuminated the interior, revealing a trail bike, several rusting garden tools and three black sacks in the far corner.

'Have a look inside this one,' Lean ordered, pulling out two of the sacks for closer examination. Robertson delved as Mrs Clarke slouched at the doorway, drawing on a freshly lit cigarette.

'What's this all about then?' she inquired.

'Someone gave us a tip off, Mrs Clarke,' Lean retorted. 'About your stepson.'

'This may prove interesting, sir,' observed Robertson. Lean glanced inside the sack at a quantity of female clothing.

'Good work, Robertson. Know anything about this, Mrs Clarke?'

Mrs Clarke stared into the bag at the assortment of black underwear, jeans and jumper.

'Not mine. No idea.'

'No. I rather thought not. OK, Robertson, take this back to the car.'

'Right, sir.'

Lean turned to exit the garage, only to be met with a cloud of smoke from Mrs Clarke's exhalation.

'Is that it then?' she demanded.

'Yes, for now. Though I'm sure we'll be back.'

'And what about Paul? When are you releasing him?'

'At present he's being detained on a public order charge. However, this may well change matters. I can't give you a definite answer, Mrs Clarke.'

Fielding a volley of abuse and a gust of cheap perfume, Lean made his way resolutely down the hall to the waiting car.

'Strange woman,' observed Robertson, who was somewhat renowned for the brevity of his laconic observations.

'Very,' agreed Lean. 'In fact disagreeable. Pity we couldn't trace that anonymous caller though. It might have been helpful.'

The Old Buttery turned out to be a small pub down a back street on the eastern boundary of Penzance where the railway age had thrown up lines of claustrophobic terraces. Inside, several seasoned soaks were gathered round the bar, exchanging pleasantries. As Bottrell entered, they turned to view him with suspicion usually accorded to visiting tourists or 'emmets'.

'Looking for the "Moot?" ' Bottrell inquired.

'Upstairs, first door on the left,' offered the publican, a middle-aged man with a complexion like dressed granite. There was a distinct smell to the pub, Bottrell observed. Dog. That was it. Old unwashed dog. Out of the corner of his eye he spotted the author of this emanation, sleeping fitfully in a corner. The old sheep dog opened a baleful eye and observed him warily. Then he uttered a weary sigh before resuming his interminable slumber.

'Hello again. Glad you could make it,' came a voice from behind him. He turned to see Anne smiling broadly at him. It occurred to him that in the subdued light of the pub interior she was somehow even more attractive looking than he had remembered her. She sported a low-cut T-shirt and he was struck by the soft sheen of her skin. She was wearing a subtle perfume which he could not quite define. He found it difficult to take his eyes off her.

'Nice to see you again. Drink?'

'I don't. You go ahead, though. I'll see you upstairs.'

He ordered a double malt from the host who eyed him somewhat suspiciously.

'You're new, aren't you?' remarked a squat, bullish man with side whiskers who stood beside him.

'Visiting,' Bottrell offered.

The man smirked and the smirk was exchanged round the bar like a secret code. Bottrell ignored this, took the glass and made his way up the stairs, to a dilapidated room where an assortment of stools and easy chairs had been drawn up into a circle. The occupants of these chairs ranged from a middle-aged roué of enormous proportions sporting a goatee beard to a cadaverous young woman of about twenty with dyed black hair and intensely red lips whose T-shirt bore the legend 'Nosferatu'. Bottrell immediately identified her as a 'Goth'. However, the person who most attracted his interest was pony-tail man. He sat, slightly apart from the others, his long lean hands folded on his lap, his eyes slightly closed as if he were meditating. In the subdued lighting of the room his skin seemed mummified, giving him the appearance of some resurrected Egyptian. Bottrell sat down next to Anne. Pony-tail opened his eyes, then someone shut the door and lit a series of small night-light candles on a small card table in the centre of the circle.

'Before we start, let's just welcome our guests tonight,' intoned Pony-tail. It was a slow, cultured voice, as if each phrase had been carefully considered.

'It is our custom to ask guests to say just a few words about themselves before we introduce ourselves to them. For this we use the talking stick,' he concluded, producing a small ebony-handled stick bearing what seemed to be a series of magical sigils. He leaned across the circle and handed the stick to Bottrell. There was an awkward pause as he considered what he might say to the assembled company.

'My name is John,' he began. 'I'm a visitor to Cornwall, staying with friends at present.' Hell, what could he say? I'm attempting to dry out, unsuccessfully, I'm poking about in a murder case I really know nothing about. I'm beset by dreams. I'm…

'I'm interested in paganism,' he added, rather lamely.

'Thank you, John. We welcome you to our circle. Please pass the talking stick to your left,' instructed Pony-tail in dulcet tones.

He passed the talking stick to red-lipped girl on his left.

'My name is Diana. I'm a Goth. You probably know what a Goth is but if you don't know I'm happy to explain. I'm interested in the Dark Side. I'm not into New Age crap. Sorry if that offends anyone but that's how it is,' she added, as if proving a point. There was a sudden tension in the room that was almost palpable. 'What else? I'm an artist and sculptress. Oh, and I have a black cat called Satan who lives with me in Pendeen.'

'Thank you and welcome, Diana,' said Pony-tail whose face was impassive. 'Now, before we get under way this evening, we normally share a short guided visualization. So, shall we close the circle and invoke the elements?'

There was a general murmur of agreement and Bottrell found hands fumbling for his. He was especially glad of Anne's hand which was firm and warm to the touch.

'Guardians of the watch towers, from the north, the south, the west and the east, we welcome you to our circle. Protect us and inspire us. May the bond between us be our guide this evening.'

During the visualization, which consisted of a trip through a wooded valley to meet his ancestors, Bottrell found himself thinking of Frances. His eyes closed, he pictured a particular day when they had visited the White Horse in Uffington. It had been a summer's morning in the early days of their relationship, before they had been married. The great chalk hill had been deserted and they had lain on the eye of the horse and embraced and kissed whilst overhead a kestrel hovered and fluttered its wings. He had long forgotten that day, yet now the memory of it, the smell of her hair and of fresh grass filled him with a great longing to be with her once more, to recapture her presence. He found himself involuntarily squeezing Anne's hand. When she responded in like manner it came as something of a shock to him and he opened his eyes abruptly to find himself looking straight ahead at pony-tail man. By the light of the candles his eyes seemed odd, penetrative, fixed with a faraway expression. It was quite unnerving. The presence of this man, and the respect that he enjoyed in the group seemed almost patriarchal. Then he turned, aware that Anne was smiling at him.

'So, friends, let's share that journey,' he heard Pony-tail say.

Bottrell wondered when there might be an intermission. He craved another malt and was uncertain about the ethics of lighting his pipe. A young man with dreadlocks almost opposite him had what looked suspiciously like a joint but no one else in the room appeared to smoke. After what seemed an interminable length of time and a dreary enumeration of the group's experiences through ancestral time, the intermission arrived.

At about 2 a.m. he awoke suddenly with a sense of foreboding and alarm. Alarm at what, though? He switched on the small bedside lamp and a yellow light spilled onto the cheap furnishings of Anne's spare room: the painted green basket chair, the old easy chair with the faded yellow chintzed wings and the chaise longue with its faint aroma of mothballs, where he had spent the last few hours.

So what was he afraid of? He peered round the room. There was nothing ostensibly out of place, nothing threatening. The door was firmly shut, the window slightly open so that far off sounds of roistering youths, much the worse for wear, drifted in on the night wind.

Gathering the duvet around him, Bottrell peered out of the window. He reached for his pipe from the mantelpiece, then passed his forefinger along its surface. Solid oak, scratched and candlewaxed by numerous previous tenants. The lighter flame gave life to the pipe bowl and a question mark of dense, aromatic smoke snaked upwards into his eyes, causing him to squint. Was it something he had dreamt? No, he thought not. Definitely something in the room. He was not sure what it was. But it had disturbed his sleep.

The tobacco aroma began to envelop his head, dulling his anxiety. He began to recall events of the evening. The strangely subdued 'moot' with Pony-tail, the patriarch. The oddball attendees. Most of all, Anne. Drinks at the bar afterwards with Anne. Staring into her eyes, those deep wells where he might rest his own tortured spirit. Her full lips. Skin like polished stone. He had been in the act of reaching out his hand to touch hers when pony-tail man had arrived and quite confounded him.

'May I...? So good that you could join us.... Where did you say you lived...?' The voice cultured, interrogative, the eyes scanning him. Was it he who had disturbed his sleep? By the time last orders had been called Pony-tail had already made his excuses and left.

He had returned to Anne's flat at her express invitation. He knew that when coffee had been concluded and they had sat on the sofa, exchanging pleasantries for at least an hour, he might have taken the initiative and made love to her there and then. He was convinced that was what she also desired. But nothing happened. Partly because he was weary but mainly because the thing that had blocked his life force for so long now claimed him and made him its unwilling prisoner. For all the while he sought his redemption for Frances' death, he could not express his lust for another woman. So he sat, smelling Anne's fragrant perfume as she sat next to him, and he cursed himself for it.

His pipe suddenly extinguished itself. Where was his lighter? He rummaged among the bric-à-brac on the mantelpiece where an assortment of correspondence and a set of keys lay with a tag bearing the initials: R.W. and an address in St Just. Rebecca's keys. Instinctively, he gathered up the keys and slipped them into his coat pocket. He stood for a moment, considering what he had done. Anne was Rebecca's friend. Sooner or later she might notice the absence of the keys to her flat. A thought occurred to him that he might take advantage of the situation and return the keys at a later date. She might never notice. A brown envelope attracted his attention with a word scribbled on the flap: 'Thelema.' That word again. Igniting his pipe, he took the envelope to the light of the lamp and slowly withdrew its contents. 'Notes On The Order: Strictly for Novices,' it read, then: 'THE PAGAN GOD OF LIGHT'.

The Prince of Darkness, the Devil or Satan in Judaeo-Christian mythology, is also known as 'the god of the sun and of the moon' and as 'a God of Light.' The name itself, when translated, means 'bringer of light'. Today's pagans express concern at being associated with Lucifer or Satan because of the past link with so-called 'devil worship'. However, Lucifer has very little to do with the Christian heresy of Satanism or the Devil. The word Satan actually meant 'accuser' in Hebrew mythology and these were once minor angels sent by Yahweh to test the faith of his followers, the Hebrews.

Lucifer, who was also the 'guardian of time and eternity' was the saviour of human kind who rebelled against the cosmic order and may have originated in Palestine as 'the God of the Morning Star'. In fact, he had a twin, the God of the Evening Star, and these two represented the sun at dawn and dusk. Thus they together represented death and rebirth.

Our Lord Lucifer is the Master of the Watchers, or fallen angels, and the chief of the angels is called Azazel or Azrael. Azazel was regarded as the father of the nature spirits or djinn and was represented as a goat god. His followers, the seirim, also took the form of satyrs or goats. In the Middle Ages the Devil was of course represented as a great goat and he was also identified with Baphomet, the God of the Templars.

So we can see that Christian mythology has done a great injustice to Our Lord Azazel.

A sudden noise made him look up. He could hear footsteps approaching from beyond the door. Hastily, he slipped the envelope onto the mantelpiece.

Anne stood in the doorway, swathed in a thin dressing gown which barely concealed her athletic figure.

'Thought you might like some coffee.'

'That would be great.'

In some ways he had regretted his underhandedness. They had shared breakfast, laughed and kissed and, because the following day had dawned bright and cloudless, walked out onto the moors. At Tregeseal stone circle, amid the yellow gorse, they had sat and embraced each other. The moors at this hour were deserted save for a solitary buzzard which circled overhead, regarding them with suspicion. In many ways Anne resembled Frances. There was the same quiet introspection coupled with an inner passion which reminded him of his late wife.

As they sat, a low cloud began to edge its way along the rock line of Carn Kenidjack, and soon they were enveloped by a dense mist. They made their way back along the footpath, both eventually falling silent. Bottrell thought that it would be beneath contempt to probe Anne for information about Rebecca. It was enough that he had removed the keys for Rebecca's flat without asking her permission. He had no need to compound his actions.

At the stile they parted company. He embraced her and felt her warm, perfumed skin against his cold cheek. Her fire was present in that embrace, but he was not ready for it. The cold that had possessed him for so long now still held him in check, so instead he kissed her full on the lips, aware of her tongue searching for his. Then he drew back, smiled and kissed her hand in a manner reminiscent of a medieval courtier and muttered something about seeing her again soon. She scribbled her phone number on a scrap of paper and looked at him somewhat apprehensively as he turned to go.

'I'll be in touch,' he promised.

'Make it soon.'

So they had been right after all. Paul Powell had murdered Rebecca Wearne. Lean had told him over dinner that night and he seemed clearly jubilant about it. It was as if a great weight had been taken from his shoulders. At least, that was how he had described it to

Bottrell. And yet, there was something rather desperate about this exalted state his friend was exhibiting. Still, it was an opportunity to share with him a larger than usual number of malt whiskies after the sumptuous casserole prepared by the attentive Hazel.

And yet Rebecca's clothing had been found in Powell's garage. And Lean and Robertson had been able to find it simply because they had received an anonymous tip-off. So what did that mean? That someone else had betrayed his confidence? And why dump her body in such a public place? It was hardly the act of a murderer driven to kill through passion – and most murders were committed for that reason. No, it didn't add up. And Lean knew it.

After the malt had begun to take effect, Bottrell lured his old friend outside into the dusk-laden garden. He lit his pipe and watched as a swarm of gnats threatened to engulf Lean's head.

'It's so damned close,' his friend complained, swatting the invasion of insects.

'Thought you were talking about the case,' Bottrell observed.

'What?'

'So close. And yet … is it really convincing?'

There was a pause as Lean's face filled with doubt. Or was it irritation?

'I know what you're thinking. You weren't taken in then?'

Bottrell blew a plume of smoke into the dancing gnats, temporarily dispersing them. Far off, in the darker quarter of the sky, an owl hooted.

'No, I'm not. After all, what is his motive?'

'Thought it might be sex. We found a number of items in his room which suggests he – they – were into bondage.'

A thought occurred to him.

'What about the friend?'

'Anne Horrocks.' The thought had crossed his mind about a possible *ménage à trois*.

'Trouble is, we just don't have much to go on. And if Rebecca was bi, Powell isn't saying anything.'

'So – here's a thing....'

'Go on.' Lean eyed him with a hopeful curiosity, his lean face etched with lines by the light of the conservatory.

'What if I do some digging for you? Unofficially of course.'

'That might be helpful,' Lean nodded, 'as long as you do it discreetly of course.'

'It's worked in the past, hasn't it?'

'True. We were a good team, weren't we? Before – you know....'

Bottrell stared at the ground but said nothing. How could he forget?

Lean stood up and finished his cigarette.

'Anyway, if you discover anything useful, let me know. Just make sure you don't disturb the crime scene.'

'Certainly.'

'And John – go easy on the booze, for Christ's sake.'

Lean wandered back into the conservatory, leaving Bottrell to finish his pipe. Here, in the gathering dusk, he knew instinctively that he had been right not to divulge his suspicions about the occult connection. He also knew that it was not passion which had killed Rebecca Wearne. She had died because she had stumbled upon something so bizarre, so horrific that she had had to be silenced. And if his hunch was correct, maybe he would be able to reveal to Lean the truth of the affair.

20th March 1999

I seem to have hit a stumbling block. Cannot trace 'The Wise One' after spring 1998. Nor Jane. It's all a complete mystery. The only clue is the diary. Difficulty is that none of her friends appears now to be living in Exeter. Wonder why?

Dunbarton had some interesting information about this

character Slade. He certainly has done his research on the man. Exeter was not only the place where he was known for his 'Satanist' activities (Dunbarton's word, not mine). He believes that Slade works under a number of aliases and showed me news cuttings about parallel incidents in Glasgow, London and Manchester. The profile is always the same, it seems. He sets up a bookshop, then operates from it, drawing together a group of local pagans. This is his base from which he forms the 'inner core'.

Found this also between the pages of the diary. Think it may be of some significance. It tends to confirm what Dunbarton told me about 'the inner core'. It is in Jane's hand and appears to be a series of notes, maybe taken at some kind of training session.

THE GNOSTICS

The Gnostics claimed that the 'light' Lucifer brought into the world was the light of enlightenment. How right they were about that. One thinks of Prometheus stealing the fire of heaven in order to bring civilization to human kind, but against the will of Zeus. Is this not a reworking of an older myth? In fact, the Bible itself supports the Gnostics' view for as God denied Adam and Eve the fruit of the Tree of Forbidden Knowledge, Lucifer it was who gave them the light of knowledge. In the fourteenth century there were many Gnostics who worshipped Lucifer and believed him to be the actual brother of God who was cast out of Heaven unfairly. They called themselves Luciferans. (Note in margin: PS: Ask The Wise One about this. He may know more.)

He found the flat above a butcher's shop on the main street in Penzance. A light rain had begun to fall as he turned the corner, breaking the almost overwhelming mugginess of the day. He glanced up and down the street. There were few people about. As the bus he had occupied sped on its way, he observed a small group of youths lounging on a corner, drinking alcopops. At the far end of the street a fish and chip shop plied its trade, a garish sign spilling its yellow luminescence onto the pavement.

Pulling on a pair of surgical gloves, Bottrell drew the keys out of his side pocket and inserted the Yale into the lock where a small electric-bell push displayed the now inaccurate sign: '17B: R. WEARNE'.

The door opened into a narrow hallway. Shutting the door behind him, he produced a small torch from his pocket and made his way noiselessly upstairs. A second door admitted him to a large sitting room, comfortably furnished, with a distinctly feminine touch. Pulling the green velvet curtains across the windows, he located the light switch and glanced round, trying to gain an impression of the flat's previous occupant. Strangely, though, he could make little of it. A comfortable two-seater sofa occupied the centre of the room, facing an expensive TV and audio system. There was also a large collection of books, neatly stacked, standing on pine shelves. Here and there, between the books, stood a number of small terracotta figurines which appeared to be modern replicas of ancient goddesses. He glanced at some of the book titles: *An Encyclopaedia of Witchcraft, Cure Craft, Dictionary of Superstitions*, and a small black volume that caught his eye, entitled *The Satanic Mass*. The latter he took from the bookcase and secreted in his jacket pocket. It might prove useful. In one corner stood a computer. He sat down, turned it on, accessed the hard drive and clicked on: 'My Documents'. He flicked through the files: poems, memos, drafts of letters and a file headed 'Thelema'. This contained what appeared to be a list of names and addresses. He reached for a spare disc and began downloading files on to it. He decided he would look at them in greater detail later. Then he turned off the machine, pocketed the disc and sat down on the sofa, closing his eyes. This was something he had learned to do on two previous occasions at scenes of crimes. The first time was when he had been left alone as a dc in a house in Woodford where a child had been murdered. He had been up all night and had closed his eyes momentarily through sheer weariness while his colleague had left the room. An overwhelming sense of fear had pervaded him. At first, he was confused by the emotion but he began to realize that what he was doing was simply picking up on the emotionally charged state of the house itself. What he felt was not his fear but the child's fear. It was an experience he had never forgotten.

He stood up suddenly, turned off the overhead light which had been distracting him, and switched on his torch. At once the darkness enveloped him and he became aware of a distinct drop in temperature in the room. He could detect something else also, a sweet smell, something like violets, a woman's perfume definitely. She was here in the room with him, her spirit close to him. He focused his eyes. From beyond the curtains came the dull glimmer of the cars as they passed to and fro up the street. But there was something else there now, a shape like a figure forming. It might have been a trick of the light, but he knew differently. He concentrated, trying to access the emotion in the room. There was a feeling of intense sadness, but also of desperation and frustration, not for herself, but for someone else, someone close to her. For by now he was convinced that the spirit present was that of Rebecca.

'Who killed you, Rebecca?' he heard himself mutter. 'And who is it you feel for so badly?'

But there was no reply. Somehow the barrier between the living and the dead could not be bridged. He sat for some while longer before he, at last, stood up, his emotions drained, and drew back the curtains, leaving no trace of disturbance in the room. Then he made his way down the dark stairs into the murky street where a light rain had intensified into a steady downpour.

Poor Rebecca. What had her tortured spirit been trying to tell him?

And who was the other person for whom she felt so deeply? As he paused to shelter and light his pipe in a shop doorway, he felt he had only just begun to glimpse the tip of an iceberg. What worried him was what lay beneath the surface.

He shivered, involuntarily. He felt as if he were Charon, steering his boat across the River Styx, pale faces staring up at him through the murky waters.

And one of those faces was Rebecca's.

He closed the curtains against the darkening day and sat before a low table and sighed. He had hoped it would not come to this. He had suspected that the man who called himself John might have been an infiltrator, but now that suspicion was confirmed. Even more worrying was the fact that he had formed an alliance with Diana. For that was her magical name, the name he had conferred upon her.

So she must be extinguished. Otherwise, the risk would be too great. He had already risked a great deal in the past. Much had stood in his way but he had been resolute in his path and he would not stop now he was so close.

Picking up the piece of muslin, he cut it neatly into the shape of a figure, then began to stitch the cloth together. From his wallet he produced a long, blonde hair and, with infinite care, lowered it into the cavity. Then he packed the figure with straw and sealed it. For a few moments he sat staring at the little poppet. Then he closed his eyes and began to mutter in a low, sustained voice. From the drawer beneath the table he produced a long hat pin and drove it into the heart of the figure with considerable force.

The deed was done. Regrettable, but it had to be.

Then he sat and waited until the candle on the table guttered and finally, like the spirit of his intended victim, extinguished itself.

Chapter Five

He had no idea how Rebecca's clothes had come to be in the garage. His only thought was that they had been placed there by someone who harboured a grudge against him. Of course, that could be more or less anyone since he had made a number of enemies whilst he had been active in the animal rights movement. After all, it was he who, only last year, had masterminded the arson attack on the Hunt Master's Land-Rover. His name had frequently appeared in the local newspaper in connection with protests against the hunt and his latest effort to thwart MAFF's badger cull had been widely noted. It was highly likely that whoever had murdered Rebecca had implicated him in order to settle an old score. And so far, he appeared to have succeeded. But why murder Rebecca?

Paul stared at the tiled wall of the police cell, the smell of disinfectant and stale urine filling him with nausea. He had given Lean a full account of his movements on the night Rebecca had been murdered. Apart, that is, for the three hours during which he had sprung the badger traps on the moorland around Zennor. He had no intention of sharing that information with the police, especially since he had been charged with public affray for his part in the St Just protest.

In the cell next to him, the man who had been moaning to himself earlier now burst into an anarchic version of 'Danny Boy', then started to retch. Paul wished he would give it a rest. He lay down on the mattress and regretted not having any cigarettes. He closed his eyes and began to think of Rebecca.

Poor, beautiful Rebecca. Who would have done that to her? And for what reason? Theirs had been a mercurial relationship. They had met almost exactly a year ago at a maypole dance on midsummer's eve, held on a hill high above St Just. It was a meeting place for numerous local pagans. At that time Paul had no particular interest in alternative spirituality. He was, if anything, an agnostic. But from the moment he had set eyes upon her, he had fallen for Rebecca. There was an intensity about her which he could not resist. It was not just that she was good-looking. There was something about her zest for life that had appealed to him. When he was in her presence, he felt alive. And when he was no longer with her it was as if a light had been extinguished. Which was why he felt so depressed. It wasn't just that he was confined to a sterile cell in Camborne wondering if he would be granted bail. He simply missed her.

It was she who had introduced him to paganism and the moot. Prior to this, he had imagined pagans as crazies who dressed up in bizarre clothing, waved wands or danced around stone circles in the nude. Since meeting Rebecca and joining the moot he had come to realize that many pagans were, like himself, eco-warrior types who believed in the sanctity of the living world. True, there were some who understood little about the sanctity of such places and left their rubbish behind, following a ritual. Metal night-lights and wax candles were frequently to be found littering such places. And yes, it was true that many of them were from the towns, refugees who had escaped to the wilds of the western world. That didn't detract from the message they were trying to convey to the world.

But despite the fact that he had made new friends at these pagan gatherings they had attended together, there were a few individuals about whom he had certain misgivings. He retained a lurking suspicion that Rebecca had a side to her existence about which she was loath to speak. He knew that she was a member of some kind of inner circle but she would not be drawn on the matter. Instead, he had learned to respect her silence.

He could not say that he had loved Rebecca. He could say that he had been obsessed by her. He missed the smell of her skin, the taste of her moist mouth. By nature he was passionate and Rebecca had been hot-blooded. From the very outset their relationship had been of a sexual nature. It had not taken him long to discover the need to experiment and Rebecca had participated with enthusiasm. 'Sex is sacred' she had told him, and he had come to share her point of view. After all, wasn't the world of nature imbued with spiritual dimension? So why shouldn't sex be sacred?

He twisted and turned on the hard mattress, trying to find a comfortable sleeping position, recalled the ecstasies they had shared together. He imagined Rebecca's soft, smooth body, cold and hard on the morgue slab. Such a waste. Such a wicked waste. Those bright eyes, dazzling like those of a dead fish. Tears filled his eyes. He wished he had a cigarette. It would be a comfort to him. He closed his eyes, sighed and began to drift slowly into sleep....

Powell was in the flat. He appeared to be floating on the ceiling, for as he looked down, he could see Rebecca moving about below him in the kitchen, making breakfast and singing to herself. He smiled and tried to call out to her, but found that his lips refused to move. He felt a strange sense of foreboding. He knew that there was something odd about his dream, as if he were dreaming it for a reason, or as if he were about to be shown something he did not wish to see.

Then the room slowly darkened, as if someone were slowly turning down a light dimmer. He was sitting in a chair now, facing her back. Then she turned and saw him and in that moment a look of such terror passed over her face that he became afraid for her. She began to gesticulate and shout, but he was unable to hear her, as if he were behind glass. Nor could he move. His hands were like lead weights on the arms of the chair.

She staggered back into the kitchen, then grabbed a knife from the table to defend herself. He wanted to cry out, he wanted to embrace her against the thing that was threatening her, but he could not. Then, as he looked about him, he began to perceive what was happening. The room had grown pitch dark and intensely cold, as if some invisible presence had crept in and possessed them, watching them.

But why was she staring at him in that awful, fixed manner? What had happened to him? Why did she not recognize him?

Then he looked down and saw his hands and was filled with horror at what he saw there on the chair armrest. It was not his hand. It was a dry, shrivelled thing, like that of a cadaver's, the nails yellow and pointed, the fingers thin and attenuated. He had not the power to lift his arm and touch his face but he knew instinctively what he would find if he did so, that the face would be like parchment, just like the hand that was powerless to move.

He closed his eyes and prayed that the dream would go away.

When he finally awoke he found himself on his back in the cell, bathed in perspiration, his heart beating, possessed by the unreasoning fear of that awful dream. For a moment or two he sat on the edge of the mattress, staring at the wall. A thin strip of moonlight had illuminated the tiles, showing a series of dark rivulets.

Then he banged on the cell door loudly.

Bottrell awoke in a confused state. He had slept fitfully for he had been beset by dreams of a somewhat disturbing nature. Dim memories remained. He recalled an open field with a scarecrow. It appeared to be a day in winter, for he felt the cold wind that pulled at his clothes and the grey, leaden sky above him. As he pulled on his trousers, fragments of the rest of the dream came back to him. The scarecrow had been strangely lifelike. Up close it seemed almost like the contents of a gibbet, he could see a yellowed skull and wisps of white hair protruding from it. And the hands, made of twisted withies, looked as if they had been fashioned to represent fingers.

It was odd that he should dream like this. Especially since today would have been Frances' 49th birthday.

He decided he would shake it off, consign the dream to his unconscious mind. Today of all days, he had enough to contend with. Two things he must do, on this day of days. Firstly he must not get drunk. On no account must he get drunk. The other was to examine the contents of the disc. And for that, he would need a PC. Hazel had one.

But first a shower. Then a walk.

The rain and mist of the previous evening had cleared, leaving a bright, clear morning. It was so warm as he climbed the hill that he had begun to sweat inside his waterproof jacket. A fresh wind had sprung up from the west, strong and invigorating. It pushed him upwards. He was soon at the summit of the hill, breathing heavily. Below him he could see the buildings of Zennor, laid out in miniature. Overhead, a kestrel patrolled, using the thermals to hover.

It was somewhere here, somewhere near the Quoit where the infamous Aleister Crowley had performed his rituals. Or so local legend had it. What truth was there in that legend? What was it about this part of the western world that attracted people like Crowley? And then there had been Lawrence with his German wife, glowering in the village, hemmed in by the locals, she suspected as a German spy. Ridiculous of course. Was there something inherent in this scarred, ancient landscape which attracted the aesthete?

He sat on a granite boulder and began to fill his pipe. Slowly the contents of last night's dream filtered back, like a dark, forbidding cloud. He had had dreams before and always they had come to him as portents of significant events. He had dreamt before the night of the crash. Not a predictive dream. A dream that he and Frances were both encased in ice, frozen forever. How allegorical that dream had proved to be. And now a scarecrow. What did that mean? A figure of a man in rags and tatters, standing in a field. He looked down across the hillside into the valley. Was it something he had seen close by? But the fields were empty, save for the sheep who moved from the hillock, gently ruminating.

His pipe now well alight, he set off at a brisk pace down the narrow footpath which took him to the village.

The museum lay at the bottom of the valley bounded on one side by a small Methodist chapel, now defunct and converted into a dormitory for backpackers, and on the other the ancient church with its circular churchyard bearing a single Celtic cross. Bottrell was familiar with the church and its curious pagan carving of the mermaid who had lured one Matthew Trewella to his untimely death beneath the waves, for he had visited it in happier times with Frances. However, he had never visited the museum that declared itself to be 'The Museum of Cornish Folkcraft and Folklore'. A pair of small stone cottages which had been converted to a single building in the present century, it had lost none of its rural charms. Extinguishing his pipe on a large round stone labelled as the 'Zennor Plague' stone, he entered via the gate and paid his entrance fee at the small kiosk.

The museum offered somewhat more than he had anticipated from its modest title. Inside, the dark interior displayed a reconstruction of a Cornish farm-worker's cottage according to the Spartan requirements of the mid-nineteenth century, complete with mannikins serving as the farmworker and his wife. The items on display had been carefully chosen so as to intensify the feeling of some kind of time warp. He paused for a moment, aware of the ticking of a grandfather clock in the corner of the room. Somehow the timelessness of this place enabled him to escape from his woes. He would have been content to have stayed here, to have occupied the window seat and to have recharged his pipe if his reverie had not been interrupted by the heavy tread of the curator. A short, bearded man, casually dressed in a leather jacket and denims, stood grinning in the doorway.

'There are two other rooms upstairs,' he suggested.

Bottrell nodded, aware of his growing impatience with this unwelcome intruder.

'Thanks.'

He ascended the narrow stairway. To his left, a small room revealed a series of low black cabinets containing a number of objects under the heading of 'Witchcraft and Magic in Cornwall.' He examined these carefully. A small wax effigy, transfixed with knitting needles, was labelled 'a witch's poppet'. 'Used for cursing,' the legend read. 'Nineteenth Century.' Next to it was a small blue pendant with a hole in the middle. Described as a 'kenning stone', he learned that this was some kind of healing stone which helped to avert the 'evil eye'.

At the next cabinet he paused and drew in his breath sharply. In the centre had been placed a large black and white photograph of the magician, Aleister Crowley. He had seen it before, years ago, in a biography of the magician, but this appeared to be an original, for he could see that it had been signed with the author's customary flourish. However, it was the text that lay below the photograph that caught his interest. It read:

> Aleister Crowley, the world's most famous black magician, visited Zennor and stayed here sometime prior to the outbreak of the First World War. According to local legend, he performed several of his rituals in the area, which is well renowned for its ley lines and traditions of witchcraft. One story tells of how he attempted to summon the Devil on the top of Zennor Quoit. Subsequently, he was asked to leave by the Vicar of Zennor but categorically refused to do so. The item displayed here is one of his wands, which he left by accident whilst staying in the local pub.

Bottrell examined the wand, which appeared to be carved from a piece of Irish blackthorn and was inscribed with a number of magical sigils whose meaning was lost on him. He had a feeling that the item was genuine. After a cursory examination of the rest of the cabinet, he went back downstairs and sought out the curator who was standing by the kiosk, paring his fingernails.

'Hope you found our little collection of some interest?' the man enquired.

'Certainly. Tell me, the section on Aleister Crowley. Is that right then, that he stayed here?'

'I'm sure it's true.'

'I thought it was just a story.'

'No, it is true. Several of the older inhabitants remember being told about it by their parents. He's not someone you'd forget in a hurry.'

'No, I suppose not. Is there anyone in the village alive today who would know more about him?'

Leather jacket had now begun to eye him suspiciously.

'I'm not sure there is. You might try Trefor at the pub I suppose.'

He decided that he would not visit the pub. At the moment he preferred to keep a fairly low profile about his activities, especially since it might place him in good stead later on. Besides, he had no wish at present to make things difficult for Bob, especially since he appeared to have a suspect. In his heart of hearts, Bottrell knew that his friend was barking up the wrong tree, yet he was not, at present, willing to interfere.

He kept thinking about The Moon Stallion and the connection between Anne, Rebecca and Paul Powell. He felt certain that somewhere in the triangle lay the solution to the mystery, yet he was not sure exactly where. Something told him that Rebecca's death was somehow the tip of an enormous iceberg and that sooner or later he would look down into the sea of confusion that confronted him and glimpse the truth.

But why Crowley? The name was significant, not simply because he had had a local connection, but because of something deeper in his subconscious that he knew would surface, given time. The whole area appeared to attract oddballs with their feet in the shadowy world of paganism. Was it possible that Rebecca was connected with some kind of magical group and that she had become unwittingly enmeshed in some of their darker dealings? He could not entirely believe in the squeaky clean image preferred by so many modern pagans to whom a curse was unthinkable and a poppet just some relic of the past. Paganism was a broad church and within that church were darker, more malevolent figures, much like Crowley. And what of Anne? Was she also part of the group? He hoped not. Anne. The thought of her sent a wave of pleasure through him as he made his way back up the footpath that wound its way round the edge of Zennor Quoit.

Low cloud had drifted in from the sea and was now threatening to engulf the far edge of the hillside. To his left the sun was trying to burn through the sea mist. There was little wind and by now, half way up, he found himself sweating with the increased effort. He pushed on upwards, his thoughts preoccupied with the memory of Crowley in the museum. It was a portrait taken at the latter stage of his life when he had succumbed to the hard drugs he so often used in ritual and when he was eking out a miserable existence in a Hastings boarding house. Yet, though emaciated, the eyes were as keen and penetrating as ever. What had been Crowley's motive for coming here to this far western edge of the Cornish countryside, he wondered? Was there some significance in the landscape? The proponents of New Age mysticism often talked of Cornwall in terms of ley lines and earth energies, yet he was sure there was more to it than that.

Suddenly the cloud cleared. He paused abruptly, unclear of his exact location. Below, the cloud had closed in, sealing off the hill in a rolling bank of white cotton wool, so that he was unable even to see the village. Above him the great rock stack loomed, like some huge finger beckoning him. He began to regulate and slow his breathing, aware that he was strangely out of key with himself, oddly unfocused. A great silence enveloped the hill. Yet he could discern, far off, sounds, as of voices, whisperings. At first, he thought it was nothing more than imagination but as he stood there, calming his breathing, he knew that the sounds were entirely real. Is this what people meant by the presence of the Small People, he wondered? Present, yet invisible. How lucky he was not to see them, for therein lay the danger.

After some moments engrossed in this reverie, he moved on silently as if not wishing to disturb whatever entities inhabited the hillside. Still, the voices persisted. At times he could have sworn he could make out actual words, yet they were not in his own language. The voices were high pitched, shrill and they came and went as if their owners were shifting about from place to place on the hillside.

At last, he reached the rock stack. All trace of the mist had evaporated here, leaving the granite rocks gleaming and grey in the summer sunlight. He sat down and reached for his pipe, ready for a well-earned smoke. He looked about him. He was sitting on a kind of plateau, skirted by rocks. In fact, it was almost a circle. In the centre was a solitary stone and he placed his free hand on its surface. At once a surge of energy ran through his hand and into his forearm, causing him to withdraw it abruptly. When he placed his hand back on the surface of the stone, the same thing happened.

How very odd. He knelt down and began to examine the monolith. It was a most intriguing stone, well covered with lichen but with a number of recesses. In several of these he noticed that certain items had been placed: a small metal cased night-light; some strands of human hair; even a tiny terracotta figure shaped like a woman. He wondered who had placed them here. Pagans perhaps? Was this one of the places where they performed their various rituals? He mused over what sort of ritual the late Aleister would have conducted at such a site.

There was no doubt about it. The discovery at the Quoit had disturbed him. He opened the bedroom window and stared out at the lengthening shadows of the trees and bushes which adjoined the garden. It was different here somehow. Up there on the hill it had seemed as if he were surrounded on all sides by the boundaries of some alien world, a world where he could only hope to glimpse the invisible entities who shifted in and out of the mist like wraiths. Up there all seemed uncertain, unrecognizable. Down here, where the landscape had been manicured, ordered by man, he felt safe.

He was convinced that the hill was the focus of ritual activity of some sort. He looked at his watch. 2.30 p.m. He listened. The house lay silent. Now might be a good time to check out the disc he had taken from Rebecca's flat. Clearly Hazel would not be back for some while. He took the disc from the side pocket of his rucksack and slipped downstairs.

The PC was a lot more basic than the ones he was used to operating at work. Quickly he accessed the desktop and clicked on 'My Computer', then clicked once more on to A drive. There were at least two dozen files with mundane headings which might have meant anything. Almost at the bottom of the list one caught his attention, headed THELEMA. He clicked on it and read:

THELEMA: LIST OF MEMBERS OF THE INNER ORDER OF THE AWAKENED LIGHT.

A number of names and addresses followed. Bottrell noted that they covered not only members in Cornwall and the West Country but also the entire UK. He switched on the printer and printed off the contents of the file.

Slowly and systematically he began to work his way through the other files. They were largely disappointing and turned out to be a mishmash of memos about the shop, letters to individuals and shops regarding outstanding debts owed to The Moon Stallion and jpeg files showing photographs of Rebecca with Paul and Anne. The third of these provided more immediate interest. It showed Rebecca with Paul. Behind them, seated, were the couple he had met in the art gallery. They appeared to be inside a small cottage for he could make out the granite fireplace behind them. And there was another figure in the background. The face was not distinct but he recognized who it was from the pony-tail hair style. It was the man he had seen on the moors and in The Moon Stallion. He was in the process of printing the file off when the doorbell rang.

Back in his room, he took out a small magnifying lens and began to examine the photograph in greater detail. It was a pity Hazel had returned earlier than expected but he was glad she had forgotten her keys since it had given him an opportunity to close down the PC and retrieve the disc without alerting her attention.

The lens revealed a number of details he had been unable to make out with the naked eye. Pony-tail man, for example, appeared to be wearing a kind of magical regalia whose significance he was unable to comprehend. He only wished he knew more about the history of magic. Something else also caught his eye. On the forearm of the sculptor he could just make out a tattoo. It was not overly clear but he was convinced that it was an inverted pentagram, similar to the one on Rebecca's body. Why inverted, he wondered? Wasn't that a symbol of Satanism? The only knowledge he had of such matters was based on the works of the late Dennis Wheatley, so it was hardly reliable. One thing seemed clear. His initial assumption that Rebecca was a member of some kind of occult group was surely confirmed. But he was still far from cognizant of the aims or methods of the group.

He put the photo back on the table and looked down the list of names and addresses. Most of them were from the home counties with fairly auspicious addresses, denoting people with middle class or professional backgrounds. There were even a number of academics on board, including a professor of medieval studies at Cambridge. Hardly your average run of the mill band of hippy eco-warriors.

He would have to try harder. Clearly, he wasn't going to get any further unless he was prepared to phone them up individually and masquerade as a member of the inner circle. He placed the list inside a large brown envelope and reached for the source of his most frequent consolation: his old briar pipe.

He had forgotten the slim paperback he had taken from Rebecca's flat. Bob had arrived late that evening, so the shared evening meal had been delayed. As a consequence, he had rather over-indulged with his malt whisky, much to the detriment of his stomach.

Entitled *The Satanic Mass*, the book was an aging paperback devoted to the study of black magic and Satanism. Despite its sensational cover, the contents were written from a scholarly point of view, the author being reluctant to share the specifics of some of the less appealing aspects of satanic ritual. He searched the index for some mention of Aleister Crowley. He was not disappointed. When he scanned the pages devoted to the famous magician, he discovered that among the *cognoscenti* Crowley was not regarded as a Satanist, nor even a black magician, but rather a synthesist of several traditions, including something called the OTO, freemasonry and eastern elements. It was all rather confusing and did not help him one iota in his search for a link.

He was just about to put the book aside and relight his spent pipe when the book fell open at chapter three, entitled 'The White Magician.' It began with a long quotation from a French book, entitled *Le Satanisme*, published around 1896 by one Jules Bois. It read:

> The screen of the choir opens in response to the knocking of a hand thrust out of a huge mantle. From the folds of it emerge three books. The wearer of the mantle places them symmetrically upon the altar in the middle and at each end.
>
> The clock strikes twelve.
>
> At the twelfth stroke, the black-coped priest extends his hands in the form of a cross. He stands rigid, silently invoking the magic powers..

Four o'clock. The flames of the great candles waver. The celebrant goes back to the sacristy to vest himself with maniple, stole and chasuble. He covers the chasuble with a black veil, a chalice mixed in reverse, first the water, then the wine. He takes also a reliquary closed with three seals. It contains three human heads so old that they might be the skulls of the first sons of Adam. Legend names them Gaspard, Melchior and Balthazar.

'Great astrologers,' mutters the priest, 'your dust prophesies. The flame of your hearts still inspires; and the more because you are dust, and your hearts have gathered the wisdom found beyond the tomb.'

The priest begins to say the gospel of St John, reversing the sense. He says instead of 'The Word was made flesh': 'The flesh was made the Word.'

The celebrant takes some of the dust from the reliquary and puts it into the chalice.... 'Be blessed, breath of death, blessed a thousand times more than the bread of life, for you have not been harvested by any human hands nor did any human creature mill and grind you. It is the evil God alone who took you to the mill of the sepulchre, so that you should thus become the bread of revelation.'

The celebrant takes the host and mixes it with more dust from the reliquary. He eats and drinks the bread and wine. After dragging the cross from the altar, he tears off his vestments and then tramples them under his naked feet.

'O cross, I cast you down, in memory of the ancient Master of the Temple, because you are the instrument of the torture of Jesus. I cast you down because you preach punishment and shame to those who would emancipate themselves and repudiate slavery. I cast you down because your reign is finished....'

Bottrell laid the book down on the table and creased the corner of the page before closing it. A coldness had descended on him. He pictured the priest with his reliquary and the strange ritual of the cross. The author of the book had commented that Jules Bois provided no supporting evidence for this carefully drawn scene. It might have been pure fiction. Yet Bottrell knew that it wasn't. It was all quite credible because he had seen it before. He had seen it in his dreams. A dreadful presentiment now began to invade him. He had experienced it before and he had learned not to ignore it. He stood up and went over to the bedside table where the bottle of malt lay. He knew that he should not indulge for he was already deep in his cups, but he wanted to blot out the fear that gripped him.

He breakfasted late, almost entirely missing the venue. Hazel, who had waited over an hour before he arrived downstairs looking grey and dishevelled, said little and, uncharacteristically, allowed the radio to continue at full volume. As Bottrell tackled his dish, comprising two pieces of dry toast and a desiccated strip of bacon, his head throbbed with the effects of last night's debauch.

Half-way through the hideous ritual of eating, the phone rang in the hallway. Drying her hands on a towel, Hazel excused herself and picked it up.

'It's for you. Anne?'

'Anne. Thanks.'

She attempted a smile but her eyes said otherwise. He took the receiver from her.

'Anne? Good to hear from you. Yes, I'd like that. How am I? Feeling a bit sorry for myself. No, not ill. Entirely my own fault. Over indulged I'm afraid. Good. About 8 then?'

Back in the kitchen little had changed. Hazel was now attacking the remainder of the washing-up with uncharacteristic vigour.

'Sorry about my lateness,' he offered lamely.

'I wouldn't mind, only I have a doctor's appointment in St Just in twenty minutes.'

'You go then. Leave that to me. Oh, by the way, I shall be going out this evening. Just in case you thought....'

'Nice of you to mention it.'

Hazel dried her hands, picked up her car keys from the kitchen table and made her way towards the coat rack.

'I'll be seeing you then.'

'Good luck at the doctor's. Hope it's nothing serious.'

She paused in the hallway.

'Just a smear test. Look, don't take this the wrong way. This drinking thing....'

'I know. I'm trying to get to grips with it. Sometimes it's not easy.'

'I … we … care about you, John.'

'I know. I'll try. Promise.'

'OK. Take care, then. And remember, we are your friends....'

'I haven't forgotten.'

He stood by the lounge window and watched as she drove off up the drive. She was right of course. Why did he do it, that martyred isolation thing? Was it the years of training, being part of a 'man's world'? Maybe that was it. But he had always been like it. Even as a kid he rarely communicated with his parents except in cases of necessity. He preferred to be off on his bike, exploring the dark reaches of the London docklands. In those days it was a different environment, a grimy collection of warehouses full of the smells of spice, animal hides and men who smoked and cursed as they sweated to load and unload the lorries. He loved going there, even more on Sundays when the dockland was deserted. Then the great buildings seemed full of the ghosts of the imperial past. It made him feel strangely alive; it appealed to the poet in him. One of his favourite books as a 12-year-old was Conan Doyle's *The Sign of Four*. Its depiction of the metropolis with its dense brown pea-soupers, dim, gaslit streets and gothic mansions where dark deeds were perpetrated held a deep fascination for him. He had always been a loner. He couldn't help it. It was like second nature to him.

What had Holmes called it? A seven per cent solution. So it was. But, unlike Holmes, he had not even approached the solution to his problem. Not that he didn't have theories. However, it was dangerous to theorize without data. Holmes would have told him that.

He moved from the window and plunged his hand into his jacket pocket in search of his pipe. Damn. He had left it in the bedroom. Instead, his fingers encountered the keys to Rebecca's flat. For a moment he closed his eyes. He had forgotten his facility to conjure images from inanimate objects. What did the spiritualists call it? Psychometry. He preferred not to give it a name. He had always had the gift. Sometimes he preferred to ignore the images, but on this occasion he lingered for a moment.

He could see quite clearly, more clearly than was usually the case. It was the room he had seen before in his dreams. Where exactly was it? Not Rebecca's flat for sure. Whose then? He tried to imprint the details in his brain so that if he came across the room in real time he would make the connection. Gothic windows again. A large leather chair, known as a captain's chair. Old pine bookcases. It was the room of a scholar, a man's room, for surely it had a distinctly masculine touch.

The images began to recede and he relinquished the keys, his mind surfacing again into real time. So what had he learned? That the murderer of Rebecca was a man? A scholarly type; well-heeled. That description could be matched by a number of people. But maybe an occultist.... There was also something else in that room. A smell that he had smelt before: a strong, cloying perfume, musky, expensive, something that might be used in a church or some religious ritual. He went upstairs and stared at his pale, unshaven face in the bedroom mirror. God, he looked a mess. He would have to sharpen himself up before the meal at Anne's. Where was his pipe? Here, on the mantelpiece. He gripped the bowl and examined the charred edge where his lighter had ignited the tobacco on so many occasions. Alongside the pipe, laid out on a piece of brown paper, were the strands of tobacco that he had rescued, unburnt, from the previous night's smoke. Plugs and dottles they were called. That was something else he had learned from the chronicles of the great detective. It was a revolting habit, of course. A sort of stench-making recycling plant. But waste not want not. Maybe that came from his impoverished background. It would have to do. He was not going to change the habits of a lifetime. He plugged the bowl with the dark strands, then topped it up with fresh tobacco from the packet. Then he sat down in the window seat and ignited the mixture with his lighter. Soon a dense, acrid aroma began to surround him, drifting out through the open window. Activity would have to give way to indolence, he decided. That much was part of the process. Whatever it was that nagged at the back of his mind would just have to wait.

Chapter Six

Paul Powell sat facing Detective Inspector Robert Lean. His bloodshot eyes were half closed and he had developed a noticeable twitch. He seemed lethargic and ill at ease. PC Symons leaned across the table and switched on the tape-recorder as Lean reached into his shirt pocket, drew out a cigarette packet and offered a cigarette to Powell, which he lit. Lean inhaled deeply, coughed, then rubbed his temples vigorously, as if trying to shake off a torpor deeply ingrained.

'Thursday 21st July. Interview with Paul Powell, conducted by Detective Inspector Robert Lean in the presence of PC Symons. Now then, Paul, I want to ask you again about your relationship with Rebecca Wearne.'

'Fine. Go ahead. Ask.'

Lean grimaced impatiently, then drew a sheaf of magazines from a manila wallet and placed them on the table in front of his prisoner. The lurid covers, displayed men and women in fetish gear standing in a variety of provocative poses. Powell stared at them but there was not the faintest flicker of emotion on his drawn face.

'Paul, I must ask you. Is this the kind of thing you acted out with Rebecca?'

There was a long pause as Powell inhaled, then blew a series of smoke rings above Lean's head.

'Please answer the question, Paul.'

'This stuff I did before I met Rebecca.'

'And when you knew Rebecca ... did you fantasize about this sort of thing? For the benefit of the tape I am referring to a number of bondage and fetish magazines.'

'Sometimes, yes. I might have.'

'When you were having sex with Rebecca did you ever feel the need to restrain her? Tie her up for example. Constrict her airways?'

Lean glanced at Symons who was examining Powell's face

minutely. But if Paul Powell had acted out such fantasies he was giving nothing away.

'Answer the questions, Paul.'

'No. I never did that kind of stuff with Rebecca. Rebecca only wanted straight sex.'

'But maybe you suggested it to her? Tried to encourage her in this respect?'

'I never did that stuff with Rebecca. I told you already.'

Lean extinguished his cigarette in the glass ashtray as if he were swatting a fly.

'I want you to look at this letter, Paul.' He drew a folded sheet of paper from a stained brown envelope and laid it on the table.

'Where did you get this?'

'Never mind where. You admit you wrote this letter to Rebecca? It's in your handwriting isn't it?'

'Yes.'

'But it's not dated. Can you tell us when you wrote it?'

'I can't remember, early July probably.'

'Please read out what it says.'

There was a pause. Then Powell read it back to them in a monotone.

'Rebecca, I'm writing this to tell you I'm sick of the bickering and fighting between us. What we had was great, but you've changed. Since you came back from Exeter I can't reach you anymore and frankly, I'm sick of trying. But let me give you a word of warning, I know you're seeing someone and that you've done your utmost to conceal it from me. It won't do you any good. But if I find out who this guy is, believe me, I'll destroy him. I'll destroy both of you. Remember, that's not a threat. It's a fact. And please don't phone me again or try to keep in contact. As far as I'm concerned we're finished. —Paul.'

Lean took the letter from him. 'How would you describe the tone of that letter?'

'What d'you want me to say? Honest, I s'pose. Most people would say it was.'

'Threatening. I'd say it was threatening.'

'OK. Threatening then. Whatever.'

'Who is the man you refer to in that letter, Paul?'

'I never knew who it was. I never found out. An older guy I thought.'

'You never found out? I find that hard to believe.'

'It's the truth. It was some guy she met in Exeter.'

'After you wrote Rebecca that letter, did you have any further contact with her?'

'Not much. The odd phone call perhaps about the shop. I don't recall.'

'Did you ever feel you wanted to get your own back? Force her into telling you who her lover was?'

'I had no proof she had a lover. I had a strong hunch that she had a thing with an older guy, that's all.'

'And you never found out who "he" was? Never knew his name?'

'Definitely not.'

'Ok, Paul. We'll leave it there for the moment. Interview with Paul Powell suspended. Time 3.30 p.m.'

Suddenly Powell leaned across the table, his face animated. He grabbed Lean's arm.

'Listen, I didn't kill her. All right? But I thought she was in danger. She hung out with a weird crowd. Occult fruitcakes. Not the regular pagans. Someone – I don't know who – members of this group – they're the ones you should be interviewing, sitting here now, for Christ's sake. Not me.'

His voice had risen to a pitch of pained intensity.

'Ask them. Not me.'

He slumped back into the chair, his forehead bathed in perspiration.

There was a pause as Lean lit another cigarette.

'Oh, we'll ask them, Paul. Don't worry. We'll ask them all right.'

By lunchtime, the morning's hangover had begun to disperse. Since Hazel had not yet returned, Bottrell thought he would clear his head by walking out onto the moors.

He opened the front door and saw that a dense, penetrating mist had descended. Shivering, he dodged back inside and donned his raincoat and a large waterproof cowboy hat, careful not to omit his pipe and waterproof tobacco pouch.

He took the narrow path at the rear of the property and headed eastwards in the direction of Tregeseal stone circle. However, his progress was made slower by the wet sheen on the granite boulders that were strewn along the gorse-clad pathway. As he reached the crest of the hill, the sun began to bulge through the cloth of mist and he was able to discern the outlines of the stone circle some distance away.

As he walked, his mind brooded on that single word: 'Thelema'. He stopped on the path for a moment and began absent-mindedly to finger the damp bowl of his pipe. He had begun to remember more clearly now. Thelema. An abbey on the island of Cefalu in Sicily. He recalled seeing a TV documentary on Channel 4 some while back. It was a place once used by Aleister Crowley for his magical rituals. Crowley had gone there to conduct black masses and experiment with sex and cocaine. The place still existed but few locals would dare talk about it even now, such was the reputation it still possessed. Maybe he would look up the details on the net. But why Thelema? What connection did this place have with Rebecca Wearne?

He dug into his coat pocket, pulled out the ounce of pipe tobacco and broached it. The smell of the tobacco was fresh and aromatic in the damp air. Plugging the bowl of his pipe he flipped open his lighter and directed the flame on the packed pipe bowl. The smoke curled through his nasal passages and within seconds he was aware of the adrenalin coursing through him once more.

Ahead, the stone circle gleamed among the bracken. He pushed his way through the sodden undergrowth, his feet plunging into a peaty morass. At length he had reached the centre of the ancient circle. Here he paused to lean against a diamond shaped monolith. The stones glistened with dew. He recalled some of the tales associated with places such as this, of people led astray or pisky-led into a parallel world. When they emerged they would discover they had been away for years. Time-slips. Gateways to the other world. Was that why Crowley had been here? Was he hoping to access a portal into another world through drugs and sexual ritual? Cornwall seemed full of new age oddballs, shamans and eco-pagans, wiccans, druids, self-styled gurus – if he could only discover the real identity and purpose of pony-tail man he might answer this question: was Rebecca's death some sort of bizarre sacrifice or had it really been a crime of passion?

He was wrestling with this notion when he heard footsteps behind him. He turned to see Anne. She was dressed in a long anorak and carried a staff in her left hand. Bottrell noticed that the head of the staff was carved into the shape of an ancient Celtic head.

'Fancy seeing you here,' she said, pulling back her hood to reveal her damp blond hair. Even when dishevelled her natural fresh beauty shone through, he thought.

'Just communing with the wee folk.'

'Good place to do it. Who knows what might have happened if I hadn't interrupted you,' she joked.

She eased herself onto the stone next to his and unburdened her rucksack.

'I was just thinking....'

'About what?'

'About these old places. And the people who use them now.'

'You mean pagans?'

'I suppose so. For want of a better name. I mean, what do we really know about their original function? There are so many theories....'

'Places of power.'

'Do you believe in that?'

'I think there's something in it. If it weren't true why are there so many stories about these places?'

'But is it right to use them for ritual – I mean when we've no idea what they were or what their original purpose was meant to be.'

'I see what you're getting at.'

She looked thoughtful, then reached into her rucksack and brought out a packet of crisps, which she shared with him.

'Tell me, was Rebecca into magic and ritual?'

'Oh yes. She did ritual along with other members of the pagan moot. Healing rituals. That kind of thing.'

'What about magical rituals – rituals to gain power?'

She shook her head and laughed.

'No. That wouldn't be right. That's … that's something altogether different. That would be an abuse of her power.'

'You mean it would be something like black magic?'

'Yes, black magic or negative magic if you want to call it that.'

'And would that be true of all the other members of the moot?'

'What is this – an interrogation?'

'I'm just interested. In the moot.'

'Well, I can't speak for everyone. I don't know everyone in the group that well. In fact, I don't really know you that well, John.'

He smiled. 'Well, we can put that to rights I'm sure.'

Suddenly she stood up and beamed at him.

'I'd like that.'

In a moment their lips had met and they were locked in an embrace.

He paused and listened, but the house lay still and undisturbed. Smiling to himself, he slowly opened the door to Bottrell's bedroom and scrutinized its contents. It was a barely furnished room with a bed, a basket chair, a suitcase and a mantelpiece strewn with empty tobacco pouches, matchboxes and pipes. Beside the bed stood a bottle of malt whisky and a stained glass. There was a strong odour of stale drink in the room. Then he spotted the clothes brush. Pulling a plastic bag from his coat pocket he picked up the brush and pulled some of the hair from it. These he slipped into the bag and then sealed it carefully. As he closed the door and made his way silently downstairs, he smiled to himself. He had found just what was needed.

Mid-afternoon found Bottrell striding across the moor towards Boscean. The sun had dispersed the remaining mist and the moor now shimmered with golden light. He was humming a tune as he walked, overwhelmed by an intense inner glow – maybe it's the peculiar magic of the place, he thought. Whatever the case, when he had encountered Anne by the stone circle he had no idea it would lead to that touch, to such an instant and unrestrained love-making. A feeling of joy swept through him as he recaptured the moment. He had not experienced anything like this for years, not since Frances.... He tried not to think about Frances, loath to break the spell. He had been so long in the dark, he hardly dared believe things might be different.

He stopped to consult the Ordnance map. A narrow path to his right should take him down past an old mine-working to the edge of Boscean Moor.

Above, the sun slid behind a cloud. He quickened his pace. Within a few minutes the path dropped into a dark grove of ancient yew trees and at the end of the tunnel he could make out the edge of a low building, the Asmodeus Gallery. Asmodeus. One of the company of medieval demons. A strange name for a gallery. He had a hunch that maybe here might lie the key to Rebecca Wearne's sad demise. There was nothing rational about the motive for his visit. But the detective work at which he had succeeded in the past had little to do with rational motives. A cloud of darkness seemed to hang around this case. Somehow he knew that the death of this young woman was intimately connected to the darkness of the landscape that surrounded him. Someone who had used her in an unspeakable way had a motive and that motive had to do with the power that lay in these ancient granite rocks.

By now he had reached the gallery entrance. He looked up at the stone lintel with its sober reminder: 'Bible Christian', pushed open the gallery door, then stood in silence, expecting someone to emerge from the back room to greet him.

No one came. There was a faint smell of lavender in the room. His eyes traced it to its source, a small burner on a window ledge to his left where stood a large oak carving of a satyr, half emerging from the wood, its face leering back at him.

After several minutes, he realized that he was entirely alone. Glancing back, he noted that the sign behind the door was turned to CLOSED. Clearly, they had forgotten to lock up.

It was a unique opportunity and he took it. He walked past the till and pulled the long, heavy drape back to reveal a large room at the back of the gallery. A number of carvings stood here, some in oak, some in ash and yew. One, in particular, struck him by the force, yet crudity of its execution. It showed the body of a young female emerging from the wood, the face blank, the eyes sightless. Above her laboured an ugly goat-like figure, dominant and in full sexual congress. For all its cleverness and brilliant execution there was something repulsive about the piece which forced him to avert his eyes. But it was not just the figure that disturbed him. There was an atmosphere to the room, a cloying claustrophobic feeling that caught at his breath. He wanted to be out of the gallery, anywhere but here, yet he had not finished, and the thoroughness of his training made him persist.

He scanned the other contents of the room. Chisels, hammers, a variety of tools and a half-full coffee mug bearing a pentagram. He picked up some of the correspondence lying on the work bench unopened, a letter marked Peter Kruger in a Germanic hand. A telecom bill. He scanned its contents. Several international calls. Some to Germany. The rest was junk mail. Nothing else of consequence.

It was as he was turning to leave that he caught sight of it. A small framed photograph. Three figures seated at a table strewn with wine glasses. Peter Koblinski, Carmilla and a much older man whom he did not recognize. Carmilla was holding her glass in front of her so that the fist was blurred. But even so, he could clearly discern the ring she was wearing. It was the same ring he had seen on the photo he had downloaded from the PC disk in Rebecca's flat. He was convinced it was the same ring. It was a snake ring, an unusual design which had lodged in his memory.

A noise outside disturbed him. He made his way quickly through the curtain to observe a camper van drawing up outside, bearing the gallery's owners. As the doors slammed he occupied himself by pretending to look at one of the paintings. But as the door opened and Carmilla Koblinski entered with a surprised expression he was possessed by one thought only: for there on her third finger was the snake ring.

He was overcome by fatigue and felt confused. It was as though there was a great spider web and he was merely at its edge, feeling the tremors of the wind, watching the myopic flies who had become enmeshed in its strands. From his vantage point he could see outlines, figures moving to and fro across the web, yet the larger picture remained blurred. Idly he wandered into his friend Lean's study, glass in hand, and began to peer at the spines of books. Legends, guidebooks, maps and some older volumes jostled for space here. At length, his eye caught a more pertinent title: a small paperback with a black cover bearing the legend *Occult Cornwall*. He flipped through its pages. It was an odd assortment of articles: bits of folklore, a piece on witchcraft, biographies of eccentric Cornishmen like the Reverend Hawker of Morwenstow. Then, at page 52, he found something much more to his interest entitled 'The Great Beast'. Since neither Bob nor Hazel had yet returned from work, he raided their drinks cabinet, where he found a two-litre bottle of Glenfiddich, kicked off his boots and began to turn the pages of his new discovery.

THE GREAT BEAST

One of the most interesting characters in the world of the occult was the late Aleister Crowley. In terms of magical tradition, Crowley strides the pages of magical history like a colossus. His learning was immense, covering as it did both eastern and western traditions. He inspired many 'occultisms' during his lifetime and after his death. Moreover, Gardner, the founder of modern witchcraft, used many of his rituals. It comes as no surprise, therefore, to find that a corner of the famous Museum of the Occult in Boscastle is entirely devoted to his life and work.

As a man, Crowley left much to be desired. He was a misogynist, a philanderer and erotomaniac. He was also, in later years, a drug addict, addicted to heroin and cocaine. As a result of a vicious newspaper campaign waged against him by the late Lord Beaverbrook in the Express, he became known in the public perception as 'the wickedest man in the world'. It was an infamy that he often tried to live up to, for he courted sensation and outrage. Mention the name Crowley to most people and the words 'black magician' will spring to their lips, yet he was nothing of the kind.

In the area of Zennor, a part of west Penwith still steeped in legend and myth, Crowley still evokes rumour and speculation.

Locals will tell you that he and his acolytes danced naked around the stones on the awesome quoit, which overlooks the small village here. Others say that he performed druidic rituals at Trevelloe. There are even stories that some of his followers stayed in the area after he left and that even to this day they perform human sacrifice, kidnapping women for this purpose. But how much of this speculation is founded on fact?

Having spent a number of years researching into the life of this man who was larger than life, I thought it would be pertinent to establish the facts about Aleister's time in west Cornwall. At one time I had thought the legend was nothing more than wild imagining but it is true that he visited Cornwall. As far as I can determine, he visited only once and that was from the fourth until the fourteenth of August, 1938. A little research demonstrated that he stayed at the Lobster Pot in Mousehole for some nights, finishing his stay at the Queen's Hotel in Penzance. Crowley kept diaries of meticulous detail and we discover that he spent most of his time whilst in Cornwall rock climbing (he was an expert mountaineer and climbed K2 in the Himalayas), walking, theatre-going and entertaining his friends, both male and female.

'Sun. 65. A perfectly glorious day. Designed Vau and Resh Atus. Greta to lunch. JBJ joined us; out to Morvah, after photographing at Paul. Rock climbing again. Wooed Greta on cliffs. She is a comedian; will come one day and snatch. JBJ to dinner, talked Qabalah and Pythagoras. P.M. at the 'Dophin', Newlyn. Early to bed.'

Crowley provides details of his magical rituals in a series of red notebooks, which he had made specifically for this purpose. However, there does not appear to be a note of any kind during his stay in Cornwall. He appears to have made rough designs relating to his famous tarot pack, subsequently designed by Lady Harris. However, as for druidic rituals, there is not even a whiff.

Does this mean that he visited Cornwall only as a sight-seeing tourist? Perhaps ... or perhaps not.

The detail in his diary about 'Greta' might seem insignificant at first sight. Yet a few years back, I discovered that an illegitimate child of Crowley (there were several), was still living in the Newlyn area. Clearly then the wooing on the cliffs had biological results. The gentleman concerned, who lived a somewhat unusual lifestyle, much like his father in some ways, was aware that Crowley had been active during his stay on more than a superficial level, yet would not be specific as to details.

Just what was it that Crowley was up to in Cornwall? It is difficult to determine this, given that historical records, such as they are, have probably long since vanished. Perhaps the answer to this question might lie in discovering the identity of the enigmatic JBJ. But until that day dawns, we shall have to speculate.

One thing is certainly clear. West Penwith has always attracted its fair share of occultists and neo-pagans. Indeed the area between St Ives and St Just is considered to be a place of great mythic power. We know that Crowley spent some time at Morvah, so the legend about his conducting a rite on Zennor Quoit may not be idle speculation. Crowley, who was no mean folklorist, would surely have been aware of the place's reputation as the meeting place of witches. His own attitude towards witchcraft was a curious one. He appeared to have a contempt for witches that was quite unreasonable and on one occasion stated that witchcraft was something of a delusion. This may have originated from his deep distrust of women. Interestingly, there are more stories concerning the activities of witches relating to the Morvah area than anywhere else in Cornwall. Could it be that Crowley was deeply fascinated by the legends and wanted to examine them at first hand?

Zennor Quoit itself is well known for its ability to challenge and terrify. One example will suffice. A friend of mine had occasion to take her daughter to Zennor on a hot summer's afternoon. The mother decided to stay on the lower footpath as her daughter climbed upwards towards the quoit. As she gained height, the daughter was aware of a low mist creeping in around her. After some minutes she discovered she had completely lost her way. As she crashed through the bracken, she was aware of voices murmuring. Now in a state of panic, she felt hands gripping her throat. She cried out. Fortunately, her mother heard her cries and came to her rescue. This story was told to me at first hand by the daughter herself and I can assure you that the look on the young woman's face as she recounted the experience was quite unnerving.

This is just one of the stories connected to this ancient place. The folklore of the quoit confirms modern day experience. It is a place associated with the fairy folk and in Cornwall, such entities are usually far from friendly beings. The most challenging of these is a creature known as the Bucca, a powerful and malevolent being who is also associated with the Devil. Could it be that Crowley might have attempted some ritual that might have evoked this being? Who knows.

Nevertheless, claims that Crowley carried out black magic rituals here in Cornwall are highly unlikely. Crowley was an expert on magic of the Western tradition; he studied widely the medieval grimoires and researched into psychology and the practice of yoga. As for black magic, that is very much a matter of definition. Usually, it implies a magical act that creates harm in some way. Crowley was certainly no saint. On more than one occasion he placed curses on those who crossed him. I can also remember my father telling me that at Scotland Yard in the 1930s (my father was a policeman) there was a file on Crowley linking him to the suspicious death of one of his former associates in Brighton, who was found floating in the sea. Yet all of this does not make Crowley a murderer. In fact most of Crowley's rituals were based on sex magic and often involved the use of drugs in order to change his consciousness. He practised a form of tantric sex in which the act of coition is performed in such a way that the practitioner heightens his magical power. He used both male and female partners in this respect (hence to Beaverbrook he was 'this filthy pervert…'). One of the mind-changing drugs Crowley pioneered was the little-known anhalonium lewinii, a substance that he probably brought back from his travels in Mexico. Could his chosen partner have been the elusive Greta with whom he spent an idyllic afternoon in the countryside? Quite possibly.

At any rate, Crowley could not be classified as a black magician, since the term is usually employed to refer to priests who are renegades from their own Christian faith and who therefore concoct a travesty of the Christian mass known as the Black Mass. In fact, there is very little historical evidence for such practitioners outside the pages of Mr Dennis Wheatley, that popular writer of the occult. At the end of the last century black magicians also enjoyed a certain vogue among French writers like Baudelaire and Huysmans but again, they constructed much of their information with the medieval grimoires in mind. Crowley used words of power, trance and seership in his rituals, and it may well have been that one reason for his visit to Cornwall was that he wished to access the extraordinary and often unstable power that persists even until this day at places like Zennor. In case anyone has any doubts about the power of such places, he should remind himself of the attack carried out on the Men An Tol one November in recent years. A local person who carried out a series of terrible fires scorched the moors. Was this the result of a spell gone wrong or simply a case of the power of the site simply overwhelming human interference? Who can say?

We shall never now know the truth about Aleister Crowley's mysterious visit to west Cornwall. And as far as we do know, he left no coven or group of occultists when he left for London. Yet it is entirely possible that he had earmarked the spot as a place for some kind of magical operation. What the function of that operation was must remain an enigma unless new evidence is found to fill in the gaps about the Cornish wanderings of the 'wickedest man in the world.'

Chapter Seven

Friday 22nd July, 9 a.m. Third interview with Paul Powell conducted by DI Lean. Also present DC Robertson.'

There was a moment's pause as Powell, his face haggard and blue with beard bristle, stared blankly at the tape machine. Lean took his time to light a cigarette, then spread a large plastic bag marked 'evidence' on the table.

'I'd like you to look at this Paul.'

Powell gazed across the table at Lean.

'I'm looking at it.'

'Look at it carefully, please – now!'

His voice had become hard and threatening.

'I've looked at it. What do you want me to say?' He picked up the plastic bag and tipped out its contents. Inside was a long piece of white electric flex.

'This came from your house, Paul,' said Lean.

'I don't recognize it, sorry.'

'I don't believe you.'

'Believe what you like.' Powell grinned at his interrogator.

'OK then, we believe this piece of flex was used to garrotte Rebecca Wearne. Moreover, when we test it for traces, we have no doubt we'll find your DNA on it.'

'That's as may be. But I didn't murder Rebecca – as I've told you before, I think,' he added in a flat monotone.

'You had opportunity. And I believe you had a clear motive to murder her,' Lean pressed him.

Powell placed his head in his hands and sighed in a world-weary way. When he sat up again, Lean was aware of his bloodshot eyes and a bead of perspiration that trickled down his forehead.

'You don't get it, do you? You still don't get it. I loved Rebecca for

Christ's sake. I'm the last person who would have murdered her, and you – you can think what you like!'

In an instant, his eyes were alight with a sudden fury. He lunged across the table at Lean but was restrained by Robertson who caught him in an arm lock and forced him back into his chair.

'Easy does it, Paul,' he advised.

Slowly the pent up anger subsided and he slumped back into the chair, still visibly shaking. Lean, who had now moved to a standing position some distance from the interview table, picked up his cigarette from where it had rolled onto the floor and resumed the interview.

'OK, Paul. Let's just imagine for one moment that you're telling us the truth. Who exactly would have a motive for planting this evidence? Who might that be? Is there anyone you can think of among your acquaintances?'

'I can think of several people I know – mainly members of the local hunt, but no one in particular in the pagan community.'

'That's not very helpful, Paul. I'd like you to try a little harder. 9.20 a.m. Interview suspended. Right Paul, I'm going to ask DC Robertson to take you back to your cell and maybe we'll talk later. In the meantime, think carefully about what I asked you when you've had time to cool off.'

Powell stared at him with studied contempt, but did not reply.

When he returned to the interview room Robertson found Lean in contemplative mode, engulfed in the smoke of a second cigarette. He had removed his tie and was sitting in the interview chair, looking ill at ease.

'Well, do you believe him?' asked Lean.

'I'm not sure. Maybe I do. He seems fairly transparent. Not what you'd call your average psychopath.'

'I've think we've already covered that angle,' Lean snapped. 'See what you can find out about Powell's other contacts. People who disliked him. Members of the hunt fraternity.'

There was an awkward pause.

'Sir?'

'What?'

'About the flex.'

'What about it?'

'About the DNA evidence....'

'I'm sure it will come as no surprise to you that it's clean. Whoever used it to murder Rebecca wiped it afterwards.'

'I guessed as much. So what we have is, well, circumstantial then. It wouldn't stand up in court.'

'Correct, DC Robertson. Hence my dilemma. What we need now is to find whoever it was who gave us that tip-off. Someone knows more about Powell than they're prepared to tell us.'

When Robertson had left, Lean remained in the interview room, staring into space. He had a deep conviction that Powell had been telling the truth all along. Reluctantly he had to admit to himself that Robertson was right. He was a good copper who worked on instinct. Despite the fact that Powell was the prime suspect at present there wasn't a provable case against him.

The family and Powell's associates had so far proved remarkably unhelpful. His only hope lay in the discovery of additional forensic evidence. He flicked the ash from his cigarette and stubbed the end of it forcefully into the ashtray.

Somewhere out there lurked among the shadows of the moon the person who attacked and killed in cold blood, who methodically wiped the electric flex then dumped Rebecca's naked body on the cliff. There was something calculated about this murder – almost as if it had been carried out in a manner designed to provoke the police. But maybe he was becoming slightly paranoid. No, he told himself, he must keep a sense of proportion. Something fresh would turn up, which might implicate Powell. He was hopeful of it.

He woke in the small hours, his body bathed in perspiration, shaking with fear. Moving to the window he opened it, allowing the moist night air to flood in. He recalled the dream. He was back in the Met. In the car, waiting for DC Johnson. Asleep in the car. A sound woke him. The sound of a man fighting for his life. In an instant he was out of the car, running down the cobbled street towards the dock, but by the time he reached the warehouse and was through the double doors it was too late. Johnson lay on the ground, a pool of blood behind his head. Although he attempted to staunch the wound to his neck it was useless. The knife had cut through his carotid artery. Johnson stared at him in incomprehension, clutched at his arm, choked, then gurgled blood and died.

He had never forgiven himself for what had happened to Johnson, never been able to expunge the experience of that night from his memory. Big bluff Johnson who could always take care of himself. Johnson who had supported him, shared his drinking bouts in an effort to wrest him from the darkness of his despair. Johnson had been the last link with reality. After that dark, terrible night in Rotherhithe he had gone down into the darkness and thought himself beyond hope or redemption.

Slowly the dream faded. He became aware of the moon slipping into view from behind a cloud. Far off he could hear a barn owl calling. How still the world seemed at this hour. He sat on the edge of the bed and reached for his pipe from the bedside table. In so doing he inadvertently dislodged the set of keys he had taken from Anne's apartment. The keys to Rebecca Wearne's flat. He picked the keys up and turned them over in the palm of his hand. He figured that he must return them discreetly this evening. The memory of Anne's invitation to dinner swept across him like a warm breeze. The thought of her bright face and the warm embrace by the old stones gave him hope.

His mind drifted as the now lit pipe tobacco curled into his lungs.

He gripped the set of keys in his left hand and closed his eyes. Slowly an image formed. He could make out the interior of Anne's flat, the dark brown curtains by the bay window, the low coffee table and the cane chairs where they had sat and laughed together. The room seemed dark save for a small lamp which illuminated the bookcase.

He concentrated hard and gripped the keys again. He had done this kind of thing before, after Frances had died. She had a favourite chair where she would sit and read. After the funeral he would sit in the chair and grip its arms hoping to make contact with her. Psychometry was the term by which it was known among spiritualists. Whatever its name, it was something that gave him comfort during the long nights that elapsed after his wife's death. At such moments he would see her standing in the kitchen, singing.

Anne's sitting room seemed darker now. He felt suddenly chilled. Beyond the lamp, the chairs and the table, he could make out the door to the bathroom. He knew instinctively that someone lurked there. Someone he did not wish to see. But the silence of the room disturbed him more. Suddenly his hand flexed and relaxed. The keys dropped on to the floor. He stood up and disengaged the pipe from his lower lip, aware that it had gone out. He was wide awake now and shivering with the cold. He went to the window and shut it firmly. Then he lay on the bed and switched on the bedside lamp. A strange foreboding had taken hold of him. He could not explain it, nor shake it off. Sleep evaded him. The image of the room haunted him, but its significance eluded him more.

He was possessed by the fear that something unwholesome had entered that room, something or someone who intended harm to Anne. Was it a precognition? He could never be sure. Time and again the visions came yet he could never be certain of their chronological significance or their precise accuracy. Their burden was haphazard and often unwelcome. Yet he had no choice in the matter. He plumped up the pillow and shut his eyes, seeking oblivion. It would be all right he told himself. Tomorrow morning he would look into Thelema and the Crowley connection. And in the evening … dinner with Anne.

‘All will be well,’ he told himself. ‘All manner of things shall be well.’

Outside, as the moon slipped behind the bank of cloud, the owl hooted again but this time it was a long melancholy call as if from an altogether darker, more ancient world.

He slept late. When finally he awoke, the hot July sun was streaming in through the window. But when he tried to move he felt a sudden jab of pain in his lumbar region. He tried turning on his left side but the pain seemed to intensify. He put his hand to his back. It was hot there as if he had inadvertently burned himself. After some deliberation he managed to grab hold of the bedpost and lever himself to his feet. It was curious he reflected, as he attempted to don his pants and trousers without bending. He had been perfectly fine the night before and he had no recollection of lifting any heavy object at an awkward angle. He was sure of it.

The pain returned, this time even more intensely. It was as if someone had stuck a needle into the flesh. He gritted his teeth and made his way to the bathroom wherein the medical cabinet he consoled himself with two Ibuprofen tablets. By the time he had had a wash and made his way gingerly downstairs, he found Robert and Hazel at the breakfast table engulfed in the smell of toast and bacon.

‘Sleep well?’

‘I did, but I seem to have developed a sort of sciatica,’ he grimaced.

‘See Hazel. She’ll sort you out. She’s now a qualified shiatsu practitioner.’

Bottrell recalled something of the kind. ‘I might take you up on that.’

‘Bacon and egg?’ quizzed Hazel.

He nodded. Despite his back pain he had developed a sharp

appetite.

After a hearty meal and an after breakfast pipe, he entrusted Hazel to ply her craft on a long massage table she had erected in the lounge. After some gentle manipulation of his arms, she turned him over and examined his back. There was exploratory prodding. Then she paused and looked perplexed.

'What's wrong? Why have you stopped?' he asked.

'This area of your lumbar region where the pain's located … there's a mark here, almost like a puncture wound. Are you sure you don't remember what happened?

He shook his head.

'No. I was fine until this morning.'

She bent down and examined his back.

'It's a weal – about an inch across. There's some bruising beneath the skin. You must have done something to cause this damage.'

The shiatsu treatment appeared to have worked. After he had taken an obligatory rest of some twenty minutes in accordance with Hazel's instructions, he donned his raincoat and boots and made his way down the track towards the St Just road. Hailing a bus, he soon found himself in the centre of the old mining town. Ignoring the bustle of market day and the throngs of shoppers, he cut across the main car-park and headed for the Victorian façade of the local library.

Inside, the cool air came as a refreshing change to the stifling July sunshine. He made his way to the non-fiction section and scanned the books on biography. He was in luck. Pulling out a slim volume dramatically entitled *The Wickedest Man in the World*, he found an easy chair and began to scan its contents. He flipped through the sections entitled 'Early Years', 'Ascent on Everest', 'Freemasonry' until he came to the chapter headed 'Thelema'.

'In 1920,' he read, 'Crowley returned to Europe with two mistresses. Crowley always maintained an active sex life and set up his "Abbey of Thelema" (a magical term which implied "New Aeon"

– but Crowley often translated it as "will") at Cefalu on the island of Sicily. For some while the Sicilians tolerated Crowley and the disciples who visited the island. These included Jane Wolfe, a Hollywood celebrity, a professor of mathematics and Raoul Loveday, a young graduate from Oxford, who was an adherent of Crowley's religion of "Do What Thou Wilt". The abbey itself still stands (though derelict) today and in the ruined rooms may be seen many strange frescoes of pornographic type executed by Crowley and his confederates. Here it was that Crowley practised his abominable "sex magic" – a form of Tantrism based on eastern practices wherein the participants indulged in sexual congress in order to enter a trance through the accompanying use of drugs – hashish and cocaine mainly. It was here that Loveday died – probably from enteritis, although his widow, who later pursued and vilified Crowley through the press, claimed that he had been forced to drink the blood of a sacrificed cat in some bizarre ceremony. As a result of the tragedy and the ensuing scandal the abbey was closed and Crowley was deported by Benito Mussolini.'

Bottrell paused, then closed the book. A child, who had entered the library with its mother and was now noisily running between the stacks, distracted him momentarily then he returned to his initial train of thought. 'The New Aeon' – so that was the meaning of Thelema. Was it possible that Rebecca Wearne was a member of a post-Crowleyian group and that she had taken part in some bizarre sex rite that had gone horribly wrong? He shuddered at the thought. But why leave the body on the rocks? Unless there was some geomantic significance attached to the place.... He stood up and replaced the volume on the shelf. As he left the library and passed into the bright sunshine he could hear the child shrieking at its mother. There was something strangely elemental about the cry. It unnerved him.

It had just turned 9.30 a.m. when DC Robertson ascended the staircase of Police HQ and turned left down the grimy corridor to DI Lean's austere office. He knocked, heard Lean's invitation to enter and was met by an overwhelming stench of stale cigarette smoke. Lean was in shirtsleeves, leaning back in his chair, staring at a large bluebottle, which was circling round the desk fan.

'You're early,' Lean accused him.

Robertson took this to be a criticism from his superior and decided to ignore the comment.

'Something rather curious has turned up,' he informed Lean, who was slouched forward now on to his elbows, his eyes noticeably bloodshot.

'From Rebecca Wearne's PC?'

Lean recalled the brief he had given Robertson.

'Yes – I was able to track the e-mails through the server.'

'And?'

'Mostly inconsequential stuff. Some vitriolic missives from Powell, but nothing particularly sinister. No, this is the e-mail I thought you should see, sir.'

Lean scanned the brief message.

'Please meet *re* full moon ritual as we discussed on phone. Zennor Quoit this evening approx 11 p.m. L.O.T.O.'

Lean was silent for a moment.

'So why is this significant?'

Look at the dates, sir. It was written the morning of Rebecca Wearne's death.'

'This L.O.T.O. Is there any way of finding out his identity? I presume he's not a bingo caller?'

'Already taken care of. I traced the e-mail to an address in Exeter. One Keith Slade.'

'So what are we waiting for? Let's take him in for questioning.'

'That might be a problem sir.'

'How so?'

'He's no longer at the address registered. According to our records he moved some twelve months ago.'

Lean grimaced.

'What do we know about this Slade character? Does he have form?'

'No. No form. According to the electoral roll he lived above a bookshop in central Exeter for about three years. After that, nothing.'

'Occupation?'

'Self-employed apparently. I checked the DVLA. He didn't have a driving licence either.'

There was a prolonged silence interrupted only by the sound of Lean's pencil tapping his computer keyboard.

'Any luck with disaffected members of this pagan moot or the local hunt?'

'Nothing concrete. Most of them seem to be harmless new age crackpots. As for the hunt – who can say?'

'And this Keith Slade…?'

'The name didn't register with any of them. Their reactions seemed genuine enough.'

'So maybe it was an assumed name.'

'Possibly, sir.'

'What about Wearne's correspondence, her diaries?'

'We've trawled through those thoroughly. One point, though. There's a year missing from the sequence – 1999.'

'Curious. Oh, by the way, I thought you should know. I've decided to release Powell.' Lean sighed wearily.

'Lack of evidence?'

'We have to be realistic. He has motive – conceivably – but I'm not happy about the evidence. It's too neat. The CPS wouldn't wear it.'

'You think the clothes were planted in the garage?'

'I'm certain of it. As was the piece of electric flex.'

'Which had been wiped clean of prints.'

'Exactly. My hunch is that someone out there has a strong motive to get Powell into the dock.'

'A convenient fall guy?'

'Too convenient.'

'So what now – we just let him go?'

'Yes, but meanwhile set up a tap on his phone. Let's keep an eye on him.'

It was six o'clock by the time that Paul Powell disembarked from the Pendeen bus. He made his way across the litter-strewn green and found No. 23 silent, ill-smelling and deserted. Upstairs his bedroom resembled a bomb site with papers and videos strewn haphazardly across the floor. The bastards have been hard at it trying to nail me, he thought. Shaking with uncontrollable anger, he sat down on the unmade bed and lit a cigarette, inhaling deeply. He could do with a drink. Downstairs in Mrs Clarke's drinks cabinet he found a bottle of cheap scotch, which he broached eagerly. Then he returned to the bedroom where he began to reassemble his scattered papers with a grim determination. He soon noted that his diaries and several computer discs were missing. His mobile phone rang.

'Paul?' It was a woman's voice.

'Oh, it's you. How did you know I was out?'

'You're OK then? They didn't mistreat you?'

'Knackered. Otherwise, I'm fine.'

'And the charges?'

'They're not charging me. They have no real evidence.'

'Are you OK for tonight?'

'For what?'

'Check your diary, Paul.'

'Sorry, I'd forgotten.'

'About 10 p.m. It'll be good to see you again. I've missed you, Paul.'

He snapped the phone shut and resumed his whisky. It would be good to see her again and witness the Ascension. It would be something quite extraordinary. He went to the window and looked out. It was already turning dark and in the east he could see the outline of the full moon rising.

It was still light by the time Bottrell reached Penzance. Despite the July weather, a cold wind whipped at his face and as he turned up Railway Street and made his way into the narrow alleyway that led to Anne's flat, he shuddered involuntarily. He was unusually trim in appearance, having donned a freshly laundered shirt – the first in a long while. His left hand clutched a bottle of fine claret. He glanced at his watch. Just before eight. He was a little early but he had a good feeling about this evening. He was just about to ring the bell labelled 'A. Horrocks: Flat One' when he noticed that the door lay slightly ajar. His police training went into autopilot. Carefully, he put down the wine bottle and pushed the door wider. Inside, the hallway lay silent and unlit. He called her name, then waited for a reply. When none came, he walked noiselessly into the hallway and pushed open the lounge door. A tall standard lamp illuminated the interior, which displayed a low two-seater settee, an antique pine table and chairs and a large red Afghan rug. The room was immaculately tidy as if it had been prepared for the arrival of a visitor. A delicious cooking smell filled the room.

'Anne?' he called again. The silence began to menace him. No reply. Maybe she had slipped out for a few moments, he conjectured. There was probably a simple explanation. Gone upstairs to a neighbour to borrow a corkscrew. By now his mouth had dried and that old familiar dread and apprehension began to clutch at his stomach. He stood in the middle of the room, suddenly powerless to act. He knew that he must search the rest of the flat but the idea filled him with horror. *Déjà vu.*

At last, he came to his senses. He glanced at the clock on the mantelpiece. Ten minutes had passed. Anne had not returned. He forced himself to act. Swiftly now, he pushed open the bedroom door. Empty save for a faint smell of patchouli oil. The bed had been made and in the corner of the room a small radio set sat on a bedside table tuned to CLASSIC FM. It was playing Debussy's *Prélude à L'Après-Midi d'une Faune*. He stood in the room letting the tranquillity of the piece wash over him. He finally plucked up the courage to open the bathroom door, the smell overwhelmed him. The bloody water had turned tepid during the time Anne had lain there, her white face like Ophelia's surrounded by the crimson water.

He leaned over the bath, staring at her blank eyes, careful not to touch her, though every fibre in his body compelled him to embrace her lifeless torso. Her left hand clutched a cut-throat razor, the blade sticking out of the water like the fin of a shark. Both wrists had been cruelly slashed. Judging by the temperature of the water he estimated that she had lain here for something like forty-five minutes. Suicide then. He scrutinized the periphery of the bathroom. No sign of a struggle. Deodorant and shampoo bottles neatly arranged. Towels undisturbed on the rail. Nothing amiss. Two candles still burned on the edge of the bath as if this had been a ritualized and planned exit.

Yet he believed none of it. Too orderly by half. Careful to avoid touching anything, he backed out of the bedroom. He found himself shaking with emotion. He looked round the lounge again and found a half-full bottle of bourbon on the sideboard. He poured himself a large measure and quaffed it in one go. Slowly the shaking stopped. In a short while he would phone Lean – but not yet. He looked for a suicide note and finding none, his worst fears seemed confirmed. On the bedside table he found several letters and utility bills. He opened the drawer and found a small pocket-diary, a driving licence and a black leather wallet. The latter he opened. For a moment he stared in astonishment at the warrant card with its passport photograph of Anne and the name 'Anne Horrocks' beneath it. Suddenly it all began to make sense. She was working undercover. What was her relationship to Rebecca Wearne? And what had been her role in the investigation? Feverishly he pulled open the second drawer and found a bound A5 book which he opened. On the flyleaf in a rounded hand were these words: 'Rebecca Wearne – My Diary'. He thought for a moment, reached into his trouser pocket, wiped the house keys to Rebecca's flat clean, then placed them in the drawer and closed it. Then, placing the diary inside his coat pocket, he reached for his mobile phone and dialled Lean's number.

Chapter Eight

It seemed only minutes had passed before the emergency services arrived. Bottrell, who was waiting by the front window of the flat, had almost finished the bourbon and to appease himself was now sending plumes of acrid tobacco smoke into the room.

'Please. The pipe. Put it out,' an imperious voice urged. He turned to face the corpulent, sweating figure of the pathologist, Don Hubbard, who stood in the doorway like some overweight schoolboy.

'My apologies. Good God. It's John Bottrell as I live and breathe!'

Bottrell extended a hand in greeting.

'It's OK. He's a friend of mine. He's a policeman,' chimed in Lean who had followed Hubbard into the lounge. Hubbard, who was now donning a fresh pair of surgical gloves with some difficulty, nodded. 'As a matter of fact, we're already acquainted.'

'John,' he continued, 'I'd appreciate it if you would step outside for a few minutes or possibly even longer.'

'No problem.'

'The body is where?' Leon enquired.

Bottrell indicated the bathroom door, then turned as if to leave.

'I'll need to talk to you, John. Hang around,' Lean said quietly.

'It's OK, I'm not going anywhere special.'

Outside, the cold night air helped give him a sense of proportion. He resumed his pipe and stood listening to the mournful cry of the seagulls as they wheeled back and forth across the harbour, tending their roof-top nests. Two uniformed policemen emerged from a squad car, stared at him, then entered the building, while at the end of the street a crowd of local youths with skateboards lounged and looked on curiously.

Far off, from the direction of the railway station, a dog barked monotonously, mourning its owner's absence. What seemed like an hour passed. At last, Lean emerged, accompanied by Hubbard. The two stood in silence as Anne's body was wheeled into the mortuary ambulance.

'Let's sit in the car,' Lean suggested.

After sketching the details of his rendezvous and visit to the flat, Bottrell told him of his discovery of Anne's warrant card.

'And you hadn't known about this?' Lean asked.

Bottrell shook his head.

'We didn't know each other that well.'

'But well enough for you to share dinner together.'

'We were becoming close friends.'

I should show him the diary, Bottrell thought. I should tell him about the disc. But a voice at the back of his mind told him, not yet. Keep your counsel.

'Did you know she was in the force?' Bottrell enquired.

'She wasn't local. We're looking into that,' Lean informed him.

'So what was she doing here?' he asked. Lean looked thoughtful, rummaged in his pocket and lit one of his endless cigarettes.

'We shall be sure to find that out in due course. Apparently, she was working for Exeter HQ. Some kind of special unit.'

'Has this anything to do with the death of Rebecca Wearne?'

'I'm certain it does. Do you recall the disappearance of a man called John Devenish about two years ago?'

He remembered it clearly. John Devenish was a Polperro man who had joined a group known as the St Mabion Druids. His interest in the occult had been too strong for the group and he had devoted his energies to what colleagues described as 'Dark Magic'. He had subsequently disappeared from a fishing boat after a clandestine meeting with a man called Steve. His body had been found days later some way off the Lizard Point. On further examination, strange marks had been found on his legs and torso. The case had been in the national media.

'She was involved with that case?'

'She was part of the investigating team. But it was never solved.'

'You're right. If I remember correctly the group he was connected with was thought to have international connections. And you think Anne Horrocks may have stumbled across a link here in West Cornwall?'

Lean wound down the car window to release the now acrid cigarette smoke.

'We shall check that with her superiors.'

'Do you think it was suicide?'

Lean snorted. 'I do not. Neither I think does Don Hubbard, though of course, he's his usual reticent self. The cuts on the arms. Did you notice?' he added.

Bottrell nodded.

'Both of equal depth and length.'

'Precisely. As you know, in suicide cases like this the second cut would be less severe since the hand wielding the blade is already impaired because of tendon damage. Also, there was a considerable amount of water in the lungs.'

'Suggesting she was drowned first.'

Lean got out and leaned over the opened window.

'Anyway, I shall need a full statement from you. However, tomorrow will do. I'll see you then.'

As the car wove its way into the darkened streets of Penzance and on to the St Just road, Bottrell watched the receding light in the west and beneath it the grey, unrelenting sea.

He turned uncomfortably in the back of the police car, a terrible presentiment threatening to engulf him. Poor Anne, he thought. Poor unsuspecting Anne. If only she had confided in him. But it was too late now. He must search elsewhere if he had any hope of discovering her killer. He placed his hand into his jacket pocket and there was the bound A5 book that might provide the key to this darkening mystery.

He awoke in the middle of the night, his back racked with pain. When he attempted to sit up in bed, the pain seemed to worsen. He put his hand to his back and found the spot: a slow smouldering fire in his lumbar region. He turned painfully, pulled open the bedside cabinet, found some Ibuprofen tablets to dull the pain and quaffed them down with a glass of water. Then he lay back in the bed, his mind drifting with cluttered images.

In his half-waking state he could picture Anne's flat. A side lamp burned in the lounge, casting long shadows over the furniture. The bathroom door opened and he watched as Anne entered in a towel, took off her wristwatch, left, then re-entered the bathroom naked, leaving the door ajar. A sudden breeze blew the curtains. He looked to the left and identified the cause. The door to the lounge had opened. A tall dark-haired figure entered, then stopped as if listening intently. Although he could only make out the back of the figure he could see that it was a male about six foot in height with trimmed tidy hair and a slight stoop. Then the picture faded and he came to consciousness, the pain in his back throbbing.

Downstairs he found a list of chiropractors in Lean's copy of the Yellow Pages. After a conservative breakfast, he allowed Hazel to take him into Penzance by car where he made his statement. Then he wandered into Market Jew Street where he found a brass plate bearing the legend 'J. Carmichael: Chiropractor'. After an excruciating ten minutes' wait in reception, he was met by a tall gangly individual with a goatee beard. After some preliminary questions about his health, he assumed the prone position and tensed as Carmichael pummelled his back.

'And you say you don't remember bending or twisting your back?' he enquired.

'No.' Bottrell grunted into the couch.

'Curious. There seems to be nothing really amiss, apart from an area of extensive bruising around the lumbar region. It's almost as if....' He paused uncertainly, 'as if someone might have stuck a long needle into the muscle here.'

Outside, the fresh summer morning air did much to improve his mood and the treatment, along with Hazel's shiatsu manipulation, removed much of the tension from his lower back. Instead of following the chiropractor's advice about resting up, he made his way along Chapel Street into the Morrab Gardens in search of the public library. It had rained in the night and the lawns were alive with blackbirds foraging for worms. Banishing his memory of the previous evening he made his way upstairs to the reference library, where he selected a large scale Ordnance map of West Cornwall. He spent some time pouring over the locations of stone circles and cromlechs. It occurred to him that it might be possible to draw a series of lines from one side of the peninsula to the other so that the resulting design looked rather like a spoked wheel – he had read something of ley or energy lines in the past but at the time had not taken much notice of the theory behind them. Could they indeed be part of some complex grid of energy and if so where was the centre of that grid? His eye gravitated to the Zennor coast. There were several promontories here, but the most central was a hillside to the east of Zennor itself. He recalled that this area was steeped in legend.

Inspired by the notion, he made his way to the bookshelves where his eye alighted on a volume entitled *Myths of Cornwall.*

Thumbing through the index he found several references to Zennor.

He turned to the section headed 'Witchcraft'. To become a witch all that was required was to touch one of Cornwall's loggan or rocking stones nine times at midnight, he read. There was more besides: tales of Madge Figgy of Raftra, one of Cornwall's most notorious black witches, and accounts of cursing and the burning of cattle. But over the page he found what he was looking for, a short paragraph headed 'Places of Power'.

'To the east of Zennor,' he read, 'the hillside near to Eagle's Nest was once known as Burns Down. Here on midsummer's eve, all the witches of the west came together to celebrate the summer solstice. And here they burned their great fires among the rocks. The largest rock was once known as The Witches' Rock although it is believed that it was destroyed by zealous Christians sometime during the Victorian age. Locals believe that the place is haunted and there have been several accounts of an enormous black dog appearing on the hill, often at sunset. There is also a contemporary legend about the hillside being visited by the black magician Aleister Crowley, who intended using the area for one of his demonic rituals.'

He checked the map again. Burns Downs. The name did not occur on the modern map. He traced a line from the summit of the hill to the coast. He had an overwhelming conviction that this was the spot where Rebecca Wearne's body had been found. He sat re-reading the text. Then he replaced the book, made his way outside into the hot July sunshine and found comfort in his pipe. For some while he stood here until at last a cloud obscured the sun and a cold wind gusted at his face, forcing him to extinguish his pipe and seek the sanctuary of a nearby café.

As Paul approached the tall rock stacks of Tol Pedn the sun was already low on the horizon. Although the day had grown cool and the air dank, he had broken out into a sweat. He regretted not having showered on his return to his mother's house at Pendeen, for now, he could smell his own slightly rank body odour. Some fifty yards from the rock stack he paused to recover his breath. Overhead a solitary buzzard wheeled in the still air. Beneath him, he could hear the cries of gulls and the dull thud of the waves against the granite rocks. He listened for a while, turning over in his mind his instructions regarding the ritual. In the small rucksack on his back were the incense burner and the candles he had been instructed to bring to this most ancient of places. Here it was that the Cornish witch Madge Figgy had once sat in the great chair of stone, casting spells to summer storms, luring ships to founder on the cruel rocks below.

The magic he would be practising this summer evening would be entirely different of course, a higher magic drawn from the Gnostic doctrine. What would he see here tonight at the climax of the Ascension? According to Meister Eckhart von Hockheim, the German mystical preacher who was both the inspiration of his group and its founder, he would be bringing The Prince into the world. He who, though in hell, could look into every soul and who was omniscient. He of the morning star.

He glanced about him, looking for the others, but the footpath lay silent and undisturbed. He sat down on a rock and waited, listening to the sounds of small birds busying themselves in the gorse bushes. He glanced at his wristwatch: ten o'clock. Slowly the memory of the indignity of his arrest and confinement began to slip away. He was still angry of course, angry at the absurdity of his arrest and the slow-wittedness of the police, furious that as yet they had made little progress in trying to apprehend Rebecca's killer. That someone had tried to frame him for her murder was plain, yet still he had been unable to figure out who that might be. He was a solitary individual by and large and had few real enemies that he was aware of, apart from the hunt members. He looked into the west and saw the evening star twinkling there. He thought of the prayer he had been required to learn in his initiation:

'Aster, as Morning Star, light on the living you shed. Now dying as Evening Star, you shine among the dead.'

A great wave of grief overwhelmed him. He had learned those lines with Rebecca shortly before her death. He missed her terribly. He turned sharply. Someone was approaching. He stood up and raised his hand in recognition. The figure waved back and Paul smiled at her.

'Where are the others?' he called, somewhat mystified, but the figure did not reply. Instead, she continued to approach at a steady unremitting pace. As she grew closer, Paul became perplexed. It would soon be sunset. Not much time left for the ritual.

'Where are the others?' he repeated, his voice slightly edgy.

'They'll be here soon. Be patient. We have enough time. First I want to introduce you to someone, Paul.'

Paul made his way over to the tall rock stack as his companion took the rucksack from her back and began to loosen the top of it.

'Look at this Paul.'

He moved closer to peer into the interior of the rucksack. It was in that split second that he realized that something was terribly wrong. He should have intuited it, of course, should have heard the alarm bells ringing when he saw only one person on the track, should have judged that something was up by the very lateness of the hour. No real time to prepare for the ritual for already the sun was dipping beneath the.... He knew now, there was to be no ritual. A cold chill, a premonition of death clutched at his throat. But it was too late now. Already the hand that gripped his arm from behind had turned it high above his back and although he struggled and cursed his attacker, and braked his feet hard against the jagged rocks, he felt himself being dragged inexorably to the edge of the rock stack. He swore then, pleaded for his life but his assailant said nothing. He was stronger than Paul and his grip was like iron so that when he felt the first punch against his back, he lost his grip and hurtled downwards into the precipice of jagged rock, in that split second before his head hit the rock and burst open like a pomegranate, he could only cry out in bewilderment and despair.

For the third time that evening Bottrell replenished his glass with a single malt and returned to his reading of Rebecca Wearne's diary. He put the book to his nose and smelt. A faint perfume lingered there, possibly sandalwood. Outside, the wind had risen and was howling down the chimney like a lost soul. A solitary bay tree beat against the window pane as if trying to gain admittance. Otherwise, the house lay silent. He had declined Hazel and Bob's earlier invitation to share a meal at the Miner's Rest, preferring his own company and the golden nectar that had become his constant friend and comfort since Frances' death.

'21st August 1999,' he read. 'Went to see Dunbarton. Found him in ill-health, having suffered a stroke recently, so his speech is somewhat difficult to comprehend. He'd contacted me regarding the recent murder in Crediton Church, which he interpreted as some sort of black magic ritual. I hadn't thought there was a connection. He has this theory that Slade's is a group somehow connected with it. The young girl – Susan Clifton – was a new age traveller, who had links with a Dutch pagan group called 'Sons of Osiris' on the internet. Found a chat room that some of its members occasionally visit. One, in particular, caught my attention – a German called Dietrich. In the course of several exchanges, he let slip a reference to Crowley's Abbey of Thelema. Apparently, two of the early visitors to the island of Cefalu went on to establish an offshoot group known as the 'Osiris Foundation' in Germany during the period just prior to the Second World War. The group was linked to ideas about Aryan purity and the notion of 'Fatherland'. Dietrich had a theory about what he called 'The Movement'. By this, he meant not a political or ideological movement, but a kind of collective unconscious that he believed would give birth to a 'New Age' of 'The Prince of Light'. It sounds all very familiar. Must investigate further.'

Bottrell paused at this point and drained the remainder of his glass, conscious of a slight headache. He went over to the window and opened it wide. A gust of air poured in, billowing the curtains. In the distance he could hear the sound of the waves crashing against the rocks of the headland. He returned to the table, closed the diary and put it back in its place in the bedside table. The rest of the diary would keep. He needed fresh air.

Outside the storm crashed and howled inexorably onwards. Donning his coat he made his way towards the cliff path. Above him, a full moon cast its silver light across a wild, dancing landscape. As he walked on into the edge of the storm it became increasingly clear to him what lay before him. Tomorrow, when the storm had passed, he would take the train from Penzance to Exeter and track down the Baptist minister, Dunbarton. It would be easy enough to get his name and address from the phone book. Rebecca had also referred to her parents in the diary. Maybe it wouldn't be too difficult to find them.

By now he was almost at the cliff's edge and the sound of the sea was like some great pile-driver hammering itself into the cliff stacks. The salt air that drove against him in gusts had begun to clear his head and the whisky he had consumed earlier warmed his stomach. He turned and looked up at the outline of Zennor Quoit, its black edge glowering like some stone-clad beast above him. He wondered what it would be like to sleep up there on a night like this. What dreams might he recall? He had read somewhere in *Occult Cornwall* about a group of psychic investigators who had done something of the kind at ancient sites hereabouts. Some had recalled ancient funerary rites, others groups of dancing figures. Such places were full of numinous power it seemed to him. They were thresholds to another world. The folk tales of this landscape were full of stories about encounters with fairy folk, of individuals who disappeared, to return years later, much altered. Isn't that what had happened to 'Jane', the 'Jane' in Rebecca's diary? She had simply disappeared. So what truth then had Rebecca Wearne discovered about the circumstances of her disappearance? 'The dead tell no tales,' he told himself. He felt chilled now. He was soaked through. He reluctantly made his way back along the footpath. Far out at sea came a mournful sound, a bird lost somewhere among the waves calling for its mate. He thought of Frances. She too was beyond the veil. Inaccessible. Yet maybe, one day, she might step from the dark and hidden world into his own.

Don Hubbard was not in a good mood. He had been woken at 6.30 a.m. by an urgent call from DI Lean. The previous evening, which had involved his attendance at a Masonic dinner with colleagues and a series of over-rich French dishes, had ended in the bar over brandy and port, so that by the time he had reached his home at the graceful Victorian lodge in Goldsithney, where Hubbard lived out a solitary bachelor existence, he was unusually well soused.

'Why so bloody early?' he complained as he hovered over the boot of his Volvo, searching for his case and a white forensic suit. Lean, who looked pale and haggard, shrugged his shoulders nonchalantly.

'I don't plan the call outs. This one was found by a fisherman around daybreak this morning.'

Slowly Hubbard puffed his way over the pebbled beach. A light drizzle had begun to fall and every few yards he would stop to clean his glasses with a crumpled handkerchief, complaining audibly to himself.

'Any ID?' Hubbard asked as they approached the body, a white doll enmeshed in a length of lurid orange fishing net.

'No, but I know who it is – Paul Powell, our murder suspect in the Wearne case.'

'The youth you released only yesterday?'

'The same.'

'Uncommon bad luck, dear boy. We'd best take a look then,' he said prosaically rather like a doctor inviting his patient to the couch, and, producing a large bin liner that he placed methodically on the wet sand, he knelt down to examine the body at close quarters.

Lean stood by and ignored Hubbard, as he went about his grim business, his gaze fixed on a large mass of rain-bearing clouds moving in from the west. After what seemed an age of kneeling and grunting, Hubbard stood up and wiped his glasses again.

'Well?' Lean inquired.

'Old chap's lungs full of it. Death by drowning. No doubt about it.'

'What about the marks on his torso and legs?'

'Oh, he probably sustained those when he fell from the cliff – difficult to say exactly where of course. There's also a deep cut in the back of the cranium – see that – impossible to say how he got it at present. I'll know more later when I get him up on the slab. But that isn't what killed him.'

'Could he have knocked his head in the descent—?'

'—and been rendered unconscious? Possibly. Though not likely. This may be a tricky one.'

'So how long has he been in the water?'

'Can't be precise about that but I should hazard a guess as to somewhere in the region of seven to eight hours.'

Lean nodded. 'Which means he fell or was pushed off the cliff around ten or eleven o'clock.'

'I should say so. But you're not going to get many witnesses at that hour I'm afraid.'

Lean looked thoughtful. 'What about forensic traces?'

'I wouldn't hold out too much hope on that front either. As you know, salt water has a habit of destroying evidence rather efficiently. Anyway, I shall need to put him on to a stretcher and get him back to the mortuary fairly quickly before too much evidence is destroyed.'

Lean waved impatiently to the stretcher bearer, then looked on morosely as he lit one of his interminable cigarettes and the body was zipped into a black bag.

'So that makes a body count of three,' Hubbard observed sardonically. 'A somewhat worrying statistic, wouldn't you say?'

'You needn't remind me.'

'So, is there a pattern?'

'Oh, there's a pattern all right. Unfortunately, I'm not able to see what it is at present.'

'That's not like you. Not at all like you, dear boy.' Hubbard glanced at Lean who seemed oddly detached. By now they had reached the edge of the groyne where Hubbard rested his eighteen stone temporarily and tried unsuccessfully to catch his breath.

'Here's something that might prove useful in your state of obvious despair,' Hubbard joked. 'Our man was sporting a tattoo on his left thigh. An inverted pentagram.'

'I hadn't noticed it.'

'Ah, you looked but apparently, you did not observe.' Hubbard joked.

'Which links us again to Rebecca Wearne. Maybe it was a love token.'

'You mean a sort of trysting badge? Perhaps.'

Lean leaned against the groyne and finished his cigarette.

By now the light drizzle had turned to a steady downpour and above the grey cliffs the sky had turned to the colour of ink. Something told Hubbard that Powell's death had been no accident. He was convinced of it. Powell had come out here at the dead of night and someone had pushed him over the edge. Why? Because of what he knew? There was little chance of proving the identity of his assailant. It had been the same with Anne Horrocks. Whoever had murdered her had worn gloves and left no trace of his visit to the flat. It had been a clean and professional murder. As Lean's car disappeared into the distance, he stood staring until his reverie was broken by the insistent ringing of his mobile phone.

'You got my message? Hastings. I've got another customer for you.'

Chapter Nine

The Chantry lay at the end of the field some distance from the house. At one time it could be seen clearly from the back of the property, but now the tall pines he had planted in the intervening years hid it completely from view. He unlocked the heavy padlock and entered, removing his coat and placing it neatly on the hook behind the door.

This was his most private place and it formed the nexus of his magical activities. On the window ledge, where a venetian blind hid the contents of the chapel from view, lay the doll he had fashioned in the shape of a man, the hat pins he had driven into its back, gleaming in the candle light. At the other end stood an improvised altar: two blocks of roughly hewn granite, covered by a slab of teak. This held his church candles, an incense burner and several magical texts, which were part of his treasured collection. In the corner, there was an easy chair and a low bedside table bearing his diary and notebook. He picked up the notebook and, sitting down, he lit a candle and began to write. There was no electricity in the room nor would he have wished it.

'In Leland's *Aradia: Gospel of the Witches,*' he wrote, 'the first pact describes the birth of Aradia and how she was conceived as a result of a relationship between the moon goddess Diana and her brother Lucifer. Diana, Leland wrote, greatly loved her brother Lucifer, the god of the sun and the moon, the God of Light who was so proud of his beauty and who for his pride was driven from Paradise. Diana had by her brother a daughter to whom they gave the name Aradia. Lucifer was both the god of the sun and the moon and the God of Light and he has no negative connotations.'

He paused and looked over what he had written. Magic was neither positive nor negative. It was the channelling of power. And here, at the far end of this ancient land he had channelled that power, made it his own. There must be sacrifices of course. Nothing of consequence would ever be achieved without sacrifices. He had sacrificed much himself to achieve the position he now held and he had done this without entering into the mainstream of his pagan colleagues. It had been a remarkable journey in some ways, commencing with his discovery of that cache of letters written by Crowley to one of his disciples in America, those that had revealed much about the magician's rituals here at the western edge of the old world, the place of the setting sun as the Romans called it. Armed with that knowledge and with an understanding of the principles of Thelema, slowly he had gathered power as a magus. And those who had stood in his way or threatened to expose him had been dealt with quietly and efficiently. He was the puppet master and he had moved invisibly and in silence. Soon it would be time to act and then the power of the Prince of Light would become manifest and enter into the world. Then all would change utterly. There would be born a terrible beauty.

He shut the book and closed his eyes, overcome by a sudden weariness. Outside the wind had risen. He could hear it among the pine trees, the rise and fall of the song of the wind. It was an augur of change. He opened his eyes, turned to the table and blew out the candle. The room sank into darkness and the coldness of his purpose closed about him.

By morning the storm had abated, giving way to a persistent drizzle that fell from grey, leaden skies. Bottrell, who had been given a lift to Penzance station from Hazel, found the journey to Exeter surprisingly short and was soon making his way across the park by the cathedral to Musgrove Row and the tall late Victorian edifice of the central library. Once upstairs, he settled himself in front of a microfiche machine and began to trawl through the editions of the *Exeter Chronicle* for the year 1997. There was a single entry about the occult bookshop for the month of November that recorded the Christian picket. It had been organized by two ministers, he noted, Robert Dunbarton, a local

Baptist, and Brian Jackson, a Methodist priest. The electoral roll for that year yielded further results. A Keith Slade had resided at 3A Tyndall Mansions, Essex Street, but by the following year he was not there. Making a note of the address in his pocket-book, he moved on through the fiche. Then at the edition for 2nd February, 1998, he stopped. The headline read:

MURDER IN ST STEPHEN'S

> The body of a young woman was discovered last night at St Stephen's Church, Exeter. According to police, the identity of the woman whose naked body was discovered in the lady chapel has yet to be confirmed. Police have denied rumours that there was evidence of a black magic ritual, although the rector, Mr John Stevens, did confirm that an altar cloth had been desecrated and several overturned black candles had been discovered in the vicinity. DI Richard Webb, who is heading the investigative team, stated that until an autopsy had been carried out they could not confirm the cause of death and that police were meanwhile making door to door enquiries.

He rolled the fiche on. The edition of 9 February carried a headline stating,

'MYSTERY OF CHURCH MURDER: STILL NO LEADS', and again on the 16 February an article bearing the headline 'CHURCH MURDER: MYSTERY VICTIM' explained that police had still not been able to identify the victim.

> Police have confirmed strangulation as the cause of death. DI Richard Webb, speaking on West Country TV's *Coast to Coast* last night, denied that the murdered woman had been the victim of a 'black magic ritual' and regretted the fact that as yet he had

been unable to confirm the victim's identity.

Bottrell made brief notes then reached for the Exeter telephone directories. There were two B. Jacksons for the area but only one R. Dunbarton. There was also a number listed for St Stephen's Church.

His luck did not hold out for long. Fifteen minutes in the neo-classical lobby of the library established his connection with the Dunbarton household. Robert Dunbarton had died in his sleep six months ago, according to his widow. Tactfully, Bottrell offered his condolences but omitted to mention the Wearne affair. He had no greater luck with Brian Jackson who had emigrated to New Zealand six months before, according to his successor. However, his spirits rose with the call to St Stephen's Church. John Stevens was retired and in ill-health but although crippled with arthritis, he was lucid and his memory was intact. Bottrell heaved a sigh of relief and made an appointment to see him at his suburban home that afternoon.

Stevens' home was a bungalow set in a small oasis of side roads between the busy A-road and a hinterland of Indian take-aways and massage parlours. Stevens, a short, burly Irishman with discoloured teeth and a genial manner reminiscent of the comedian Dave Allen, invited Bottrell into his inner sanctum, a cosy miscellany of threadbare chairs, lounging cats and piles of fading newspapers. He recalled the St Stephen's Church murder well. Bottrell felt a glow of inner satisfaction as Stevens plied him with tea and sat opposite him in a rickety cane chair, stoppering his pipe with coarse tobacco, which he then lit with vigour.

'I kept all the news cuttings for that period,' he observed as his head became wreathed in a cloud of pungent tobacco smoke. Bottrell, who was sitting opposite, eyed him attentively, his pipe also flamed and freshly lit.

'They're all up there under S,' he added, indicating a series of box files, stacked on the groaning Victorian mantelpiece.

'Good old index,' Bottrell mused, recalling Holmes's own irregular index system. He could hardly believe the turn in his fortunes. Stevens staggered to his feet with the aid of a bone-handled walking stick and pulled the box file from its position on the shelf. Bottrell leafed through the pages of the file. To his disappointment the reports on the murdered girl shared much that was the same.

'One of the reports stated that you found evidence there'd been some sort of ritual in the church,' Bottrell offered.

'That's right, though the police weren't too keen on my mentioning it to the media as I recall.' Stevens shrugged his shoulders.

'Frankly, nothing surprised me during my incumbency. We had drug addicts in the churchyard, youths fornicating on the tombstones or throwing up on Christmas Eve at the back of the church. You name it, we had it!'

'So what did you find?'

'Someone had fouled the altar cloth. It was drenched in urine. Also, there was black candle wax on the altar. Oh, and a strange odour in the Lady Chapel – a sort of sulphurous smell. Quite revolting. I shall never forget it.'

'And do you think her death had anything to do with black magic?'

'Quite possibly. I wouldn't count anything out these days.'

'You found her when?'

'The Saturday evening.'

'February 1st?'

'I don't recall the exact date. Yes, that was probably it, February 1st. It was a shock to the system, I can tell you. I'd gone in to set out the parish newsletter and the new hymn books. It was the smell from the Lady Chapel that aroused my suspicions. When I pulled back the curtain and I looked, there she was....'

'How was she exactly?' Bottrell pressed him.

'Stark naked of course laid out on the altar. Spread-eagled on her back. A lovely looking girl. Such a tragedy. Her eyes staring like that. It … upset me, her being there.'

His eyes began to fill with the memory of the event.

'Do you remember anything else, any detail which might be of help?'

'Look, Mr Bottrell—'

'John. The name's John.'

'All right. John then. You've explained to me that you're a policeman but why dig all this up now? It's history, isn't it? Done and dusted.'

'Far from it. It's an unexplained murder – an open file – a cold case – we don't even know the victim's identity.'

Stevens looked puzzled.

'What do you mean? Of course, the police knew who she was. Look here.'

He reached for the file and began to turn the pages. Bottrell stared in astonishment, removing the pipe from his lips. There was a short silence while Stevens stared first at Bottrell, then at the news cutting.

'I thought you knew,' he said at last. Bottrell did not reply. Instead, he sat silently reading and re-reading the line of the article from the *Devon Chronicle* dated September 1997. 'The murdered girl whose identity has now been confirmed as one Jane Wearne....' In that brief moment, which seemed like an age, the truth dawned on him. Wearne, Jane Wearne.

Bottrell had intended to return to Penzance the same evening but the lead Stevens had provided for him had proved so useful he decided to check into a nearby b. & b. and resume his investigation the following morning. Clutching an envelope containing the news cuttings Stevens had shown him earlier, he left the smoke laden bungalow and made his way down a street congested with suited businessmen and rush hour traffic. Two streets on he found himself in a narrow back street of terraced Victorian villas where he found refuge in a dingy pub bearing the foliate head of The Green Man. Weary with the stale air of the city, he entered and found inside a seedy bar where two bullet-headed workmen were plying a middle-aged prostitute with drinks. The woman, whose plump figure was barely concealed by a tight leather miniskirt, smiled invitingly to him as Bottrell entered, but the smile, which was toothless, and the grey flesh of her cadaverous face repulsed him. Behind the bar a middle-aged landlord with watery eyes stared at him as if he were an alien entering passport control at an airport.

'I'd like a room for the night if that's possible?' Bottrell enquired.

'I've got one single left. Forty quid. Full English,' came the laconic reply. Bottrell stared as the cigarette on his lower lip sprayed ash along the fake marble bar and accepted his fate without reply.

The room was no worse and no better than he had imagined. A stale smell of someone else's body odour lingered there and the crumpled bed had not been made from the previous occupancy. He went over to the window and tried to force it open but without success for it had been painted in. Cursing his luck he reached for his hip flask and filled it from the half bottle of Teacher's whisky he had been forced to purchase in the bar. Although the whisky tasted bland by comparison with the malt that was his usual tipple, he downed it with alacrity and began dialling the number Stevens had given him for Jane Wearne's parents' home. A woman with an Asian accent answered but was unable to help him. It was evident that the Wearnes had not lived there for some years. He sat on the edge of the bed figuring out what to do. In the morning he would check the Exeter electoral role. Meanwhile, he had a date with oblivion aided by his hip flask. Not bothering to undress, he lay back on the stained pillow and thought of happier, earlier times. Frances laughing, running along the beach at Sennen Cove, her long golden hair flowing in the wind. Outside, the Exeter night breathed its sulphurous grey breath on the city's inhabitants.

The following morning a walk on the cathedral green soon dispersed his hangover and the grim memory of the pub. With some reluctance he left the bright sunshine and open spaces to plunge into the neon-lit interior of the reference library. Here the electoral records confirmed that by 1997 Mr and Mrs Wearne were no longer resident at Laburnum Street, which he discovered was on the eastern perimeter of the city. The present occupants were a Mr and Mrs Gill. A second phone call to Mrs Gill procured for Bottrell the name of the estate agent who had sold the property and a third provided a lucky break. The agent recalled his client well. Mrs Wearne was a widow who had suffered from Alzheimer's disease and had been forced to sell the property to finance her entry into a private nursing home. Mrs Wearne's solicitor was equally forthcoming. She had been admitted to St Saviour's Nursing Home in Blenheim Street in late 1996.

Bottrell discovered St Saviour's Nursing Home to be a tall imposing Edwardian mansion in a maze of streets behind Exeter prison. He mounted the flight of steps that led up to its neo-classical porch and pressed the intercom switch. A woman's cheery voice in a thick Irish brogue invited him to enter. Explaining the nature of his visit to Sister O'Leary, as she wished to be known, he entered a large living room crowded with aged women, some dozing, others staring absently out of the double glazed windows on to an area of disorderly rose gardens at the back. Audrey Wearne, he soon discovered, rarely socialized with the other inmates and was in a room at the top where she was presently entertaining a visitor.

He signed the visitor's book and mounted the staircase. He found Audrey Wearne in a large airy room at the back of the property. Audrey was sitting up in bed, a tiny skeletal woman with large absent eyes.

'Who's this?' she blurted as he entered. 'Who is it?'

The petite young woman who sat by her bed looked at Bottrell in a challenging manner and he quickly introduced himself. The old lady soon lost interest and began mumbling to herself.

'Debbie Hunt,' the young woman introduced herself, smiling and offering a long, pale hand. Bottrell smiled back. 'I'm a friend of the family.' She glanced at Audrey Wearne. 'I suppose you've come to ask her about Jane. I'm afraid you won't get very far. You see Audrey's a bit confused. She's been like this since before Rebecca died.'

'You knew Jane and Rebecca?'

'I was Jane's best friend. Had been since we were at school together in Exeter.'

By now Audrey had begun to stare and point at Bottrell as if alarmed by his continued presence.

'Perhaps we should talk outside,' Bottrell suggested.

On the train back to Penzance, Bottrell poured over the documents Debbie Hunt had given him and the contents of their brief, but valuable, meeting over cappuccinos in an Exeter café. He had discovered that she had been Jane Wearne's old and closest friend until the time of her disappearance. They had attended the same secondary school together and both had subsequently gone to Exeter University where they studied for degrees in history and anthropology. It was here that they had discovered paganism through a university pagan moot. Bottrell listened carefully as Debbie explained their joint quest for spirituality, commencing with alternative medicine, tai chi and later (in their second year) their participation in a Gardnerian wiccan group that held its rituals in a large house in suburban Exeter. Debbie explained to Bottrell that she, like Jane, had been initiated as a wiccan but had grown uneasy with the Gardnerian insistence on flagellation among other members of the group. Subsequently, she had left the group and had become a solitary hedge witch but had retained her friendship with Jane. During the summer vacation of 1996 she had lost contact with Jane but by the autumn of that year, she understood from conversations with her friend that she had found a new group, which had its headquarters over an occult bookshop in central Exeter.

'She didn't speak about it very much,' she told Bottrell. 'It puzzled me. We'd always shared everything. But in those days she'd changed a lot. Jane was always a bubbly, outgoing sort of person you see but she'd become withdrawn – much more serious.'

'When you asked her about the group did she tell you anything about the leader of the group, Keith Slade? Did you ever meet him?'

'She never mentioned him except the once. She called him the master. What worried me about this group was the stuff they were dealing with.'

'What do you mean exactly?

'I mean what they were into. Jane gave me a leaflet about the group once. When I read it, it had a load of material about Aleister Crowley, his Abbey of Thelema and someone called "The Prince".'

Bottrell nodded. 'Go on.'

'It was pretty dark. Black magic people used to call it in the 1950s. You know. All that Dennis Wheatley stuff. I told Jane I thought it was dangerous for her to be involved in a group like that. Satanists I called them. She became angry and told me to mind my own business. After that, I rather lost touch with her. I had a bad feeling about that group. As it happens I suppose I was proved right.'

'And Rebecca? How well did you know her?'

'Not very well. I met her about four times after that, I guess. She would visit Jane when she was up at university. She was more worldly than Jane, more down to earth really.'

'Did you voice your fears about Jane to her?'

'Of course – in fact, I was the one who drew her attention to what was going on. After Jane had died she came to see me in my postgraduate year a couple of times. She told me the police weren't taking the occult angle very seriously. She was frustrated about that, angry. You also have to remember that Jane's death had a terrible effect on her parents. You know that her dad committed suicide?'

'I had no idea.'

'After he died, her mum became very depressed. Shortly after that she developed the Alzheimer's and was forced to sell the house. I went down to see Audrey at that time to give her a bit of support. I wasn't going to give up on her. That's when I discovered Jane's Book of Shadows.'

'Book of what?' Bottrell interrupted.

'Book of Shadows. Audrey and I found it among her university stuff when we'd cleared her room out. She'd disappeared, you see, at the end of term. We all thought she'd gone off with her old boyfriend Peter during the summer recess, but when the new term started and she still hadn't shown up, the alarm bells began to ring. The odd thing is that someone had broken into her room during the recess. Most of her stuff had been turned upside-down but nothing much was actually missing. The TV, CD player, her jewellery, that stuff was all still intact. However, a personal file had gone missing and some of her computer stuff had been removed. But the Book of Shadows was still there. I remembered where she kept it, you see. We both had a Book of Shadows, both kept our innermost thoughts in that book. I still use mine even now.'

Bottrell leaned forward in the chair. 'I don't suppose you still have Jane's book?'

'Naturally, I kept it. It's one of the few things I have left to remind me of Jane. You're welcome to borrow it of course as long as you promise to return it.'

Bottrell smiled. 'I promise.'

He arrived only just in time at Exeter station to catch the six o'clock train back to Penzance. The carriages were unusually crowded with rush hour commuters and he was forced to stand most of the way, sardined between two large drinking football fans and an uneasy looking Asian businessman who sweated profusely in the oppressive late July heat. When he arrived, Penzance station was alive with families of tourists, who were beset by a group of disconsolate beggars, as they exited into a wild cacophony of seagulls and rush hour traffic. A sudden hunger overwhelming him, Bottrell headed for a fish and chip shop opposite the harbour where he sated his ravenous appetite, swilling down the flabby chips he had purchased with a can of sugary coke. He hailed a taxi and was soon winding his way out on to the moors beyond Tremethick Cross, the window down, inhaling the clean sharp air of the Atlantic ocean. It had all begun in Exeter, he mused, flipping through the pages of Jane's Book of Shadows. Some dark shadow had formed there and moved inexorably westwards and now it was here it had claimed the lives of three people. Though why they had died was still a mystery to him, he was just beginning to build a picture of the perverse ideology that had inspired their killer.

It was only a matter of time before he would piece together the final sections of the jigsaw. There was no doubt that the answer lay here somewhere in this ancient and enigmatic landscape.

His thoughts were brought to an abrupt conclusion as the taxi slid to a halt in a queue of holiday traffic. A traffic policeman leaned in over the driver's door, his face bathed in sweat.

'Sorry mate. This is going to take a while.'

'What's the problem officer?'

'Three car collision plus a jack-knifed lorry I'm afraid. It'll take several hours before we sort it.'

Bottrell tapped on the sliding door.

'It's OK driver. You can drop me here, I'll walk the rest of the way.'

Once off the road, the stench of petrol fumes began to recede and he was able to make his way down a hawthorn-lined footpath, which wound its way eventually to a higher gradient and across open moorland. The keen Atlantic wind billowed his clothes and far off in the direction of Chun Quoit, he could hear the mournful cry of the buzzard as its circled above its prey. The sun, now low on the horizon, had disappeared behind a bank of dark cloud and the mood of the moorland began to shift subtly and disconcertingly. He became aware of how alone he was up here. On all sides, the weathered and worn shapes of nature gathered like silent sentinels. He began to feel that he was being watched and he quickened his pace, aware that a low mist had gathered, enveloping the bushes and grey lichened stones. By now he was within a few hundred yards of Chun Quoit, that commanding and solitary place of ancient burial with its curious flat capstone. A light rain was falling and, feeling weary, he decided he would take advantage of the place and shelter in its dry interior.

Once inside, he squatted on his haunches and, reaching for his pipe and tobacco pouch, he was soon inhaling the aromatic, acrid smoke. The faint unease that had troubled him on the St Just road seemed stronger than ever now and, try as he might to dispel it, he found himself on edge, more watchful than usual. The rain was sweeping across the moorland in broad vertical swathes and the summer sky was an inky black, huge plumes of rain bearing clouds moving in rapidly from the west. The fatigue of his long journey began to overtake him and, leaning back against one of the great granite uprights, he gave way to fatigue and closed his eyes momentarily, allowing the dense tobacco smoke to curl a slow path through his nostrils lulling him into sleep.

Time passed. When or how he had drifted off into sleep he could not be sure afterwards but when he came to, it was with a rude awakening. When he opened his eyes a dense shadow appeared to have fallen across the entry to the tomb. Before he could react, within an instant a hand reached in and grasped him by the throat. He had only seconds to think. He was wide awake now and fighting for his life, for the hand that gripped and choked the life from him was broad and powerful. Against the outline of the quoit he could see nothing but the dark outline of the head that appeared to him, which was masked and eyeless. Unable to breathe, he tried to raise himself to his feet but he slipped on the wet rock and fell back, banging his head in the process. The figure was on him now. He could hear its deep stentorian breath, smell its strange earthy odour, its damp clothes flapping about him like bat's wings. His strength was leaching away from him now; there were stars before his eyes and his strength was all but gone. With one last, desperate attempt he gripped his door keys and drove them deep into the flesh of the body that pinned him down. There was a sudden sharp cry of pain and then the figure recoiled. Seeing his chance, Bottrell staggered to his feet and, levering himself with his arms against the granite uprights, he lashed out with his feet, delivering a sharp crack to his attacker's legs.

Once outside, for a long while, he stood leaning against the quoit, drinking in great lungfuls of air, his body trembling. He could see nothing ahead, for the mist had closed in now and enveloped his attacker, drawing him back into the darkness from whence he had sprung. After what seemed an eternity he picked up his pipe and, gathering his rain-drenched jacket about him, he made his way down the narrow gorse girt path until at long last he could make out the lights of the farmhouse ahead.

Chapter Ten

The incident on the moor had shaken him more than he was prepared to admit. Until now he had imagined that he had been immune from the threat that had terminated the lives of Rebecca and Jane Wearne and Anne Horrocks but it was now evident that he was in danger and that his movements were being minutely watched. He wondered if the excruciating pains in his back also had something to do with what had happened in the quoit. Someone had spotted him on the moorland footpath or even more likely trailed him from the railway station. He suspected it must have been the sculptor, Peter Koblinski. In the morning perhaps he might talk to Bob Lean and ask what progress had been made on the case or maybe he would pay a visit to the gallery.

Pouring himself a large malt, he removed his sodden clothes and laid them out to dry over the bedhead. Then he donned a bathrobe and, turning on the bedside lamp, he sat down in the cane chair by the window and opened Jane Wearne's Book of Shadows. The first entry was Samhain, dated 1995 and gave a few personal details about Jane's early years, her university days and her links with the Exeter pagan moot. There was a checklist of its members (thirteen in all) with addresses provided including those of Peter and Carmilla Koblinski, the gallery owners. These he copied into a small notebook, thinking that they might prove useful. The next few pages described Jane's initiation into wicca and some of her misgivings about the Gardnerian tradition. Then, in late December 1995, a new name appeared. It seemed that Jane had attended a meeting at the occult bookshop in Exeter where she had met Keith Slade and other members of the 'Brethren of the Morning Star'. From her account, Slade seemed to her powerful and charismatic. From then on she had attended several of their meetings, achieving in due course the status of 'sister'. There were several oblique references to rituals but these were somewhat gnomic in fashion. Then on 20th January 1996 he found this account in an altogether different hand:

Order of the ceremony of the initiation of Brethren of the Morning Star. Three rooms are required. First is The Black Room. The apartment is hung in black. There is an altar and a 'super-altar' with three steps. Its cover is black with a white border. Five swords are embroidered on the frontal in white or silver. Beside the altar on the right is a throne for the MWS (Most Wise Sovereign). On the left is a second throne for the Prelate. The Black Room opens into the Chamber of Death, which in turn gives upon the Red Room. It is furnished with emblems of mortality. There is a figure in a winding sheet laid out as a corpse. Behind this emblem is a lamp charged with spirits of wine and salt. There are seven flambeaux fixed in skulls and crossbones. The Red Room is hung with red and contains a ladder with seven steps. On each step are movable letters, FHCINRI. Each letter is covered with a candle. Here follows the order of words:

First Guard: The ninth hour of the day.
The Sovereign: It is the hour when the veil of the Temple was rent asunder and darkness overspread the earth, when the True Light came upon the earth and the word was lost.
The Sovereign: May the benign influence of the Prince of the Morning Light prosper our endeavour to recover the lost word. For this purpose I declare this Chapter of the Brethren of the Morning Light duly open in the name of the great Lucifer.

The candidate then promises to undertake the journey from darkness into light and, kneeling before the MWS, takes a solemn oath never to reveal the secrets or mysteries of the Brethren.

The second point marks the beginning of a journey through the Valley of Death. This is represented by the Black Room, which is in a state of chaos. He is left alone here but is presently accompanied by Behemoth who conducts him through the Valley of Death to the Mansions of

Bliss. The candidate then climbs the ladder on the steps of which he discovers the remaining letters of the Lost Word. He is then greeted by the MWS, 'In the name of Him who is the Word.' The candidate is then invested with the collar and jewel of the Order, a single pentagram is engraved upon his thigh, and is proclaimed by the Herald. The candidate is then invited to break bread and eat salt with the brethren, pledging to each other their fidelity and friendship and invoking the blessing of the Prince of Light. The Prelate then takes a chalice containing wine and salt. He puts the 'rod' in the chalice and the spirit is lighted.

The Prelate: Consummatum est.

The MWS: This chapter is now closed, in the name of the Prince of the Morning Star. Depart in peace.

Bottrell looked up from the book and glanced at his watch. Ten past midnight. He felt weary and his back ached. Lying back on the bed he pondered what he had just read. So this had been the initiation of Jane Wearne. Where had the journey led her? Through the Valley of Death? And what had been the ultimate aim of the one who called himself 'The Most Wise Sovereign?' Maybe he was about to find that out.

Lean did not arrive home until way past midnight. By this time Bottrell had slipped into a profound slumber, his half-empty glass edging its yellow stain onto the crumpled bed sheet about him.

It had been a busy day. The autopsy on Powell had revealed that although the cause of death was drowning, he had sustained severe injuries to the back, legs and cranium. There were no contact traces on the body and there had been no witness to what was undoubtedly an act of premeditated murder. Powell's parents, who had identified the body earlier, had been unusually co-operative to DC Robertson who had subsequently conducted a scrupulous final search of Powell's effects. Among his belongings he had discovered a small pocket book, giving details of an organization known as The Brethren of the Morning Star. Among the names listed as members were those of Peter and Carmilla Koblinski, and one Jane Wearne. There was also a reference to someone known as MWS who was elsewhere termed 'The Master'.

DC Robertson said, 'I checked the name of the group on Holmes. It appears that the group was originally established in the USA around 1950. Its beliefs and practices are based on the writings of Aleister Crowley, the black magician. Crowley was notorious for....'

'No need to elaborate. I've heard of him,' Lean snapped impatiently.

'Sorry sir – anyway, it seems that several of the organizations, quasi-Masonic in style, established themselves in various European countries in the mid-50s. Interpol, who had quite a large file on them, refer to them as Satanists, though the group deny they are anything of the kind. In 1975 the Home Office banned one of their leading members from visiting Britain because the organization was then classified as a cult.'

'And he is?'

'Was – one James Selkirk. No good to us though I'm afraid. He died in 1985.'

'Links with the West Country?'

'There was a lodge established in Exeter in the early 1990s, but it appears to have concluded business by around 1996.'

'So why was Anne Horrocks still investigating the Devon angle?'

'Exeter police have confirmed she was looking into the death of Jane Wearne. She had been part of the original undercover operation assigned to investigate the cult in the late 80s. By the early 90s the group was no longer deemed dangerous, so it wasn't thought necessary to assign the case to more than one undercover officer.'

'None of this surprises me,' said Lean nonchalantly. 'Did you dig up anything else useful? Anything we could use as evidence?'

Robertson bit his lip in suppressed annoyance then placed Powell's pocketbook on the table.

'What's this?'

'Powell's book of ideas and notes.'

'Anything we can actually use?'

'As regards concrete evidence, nothing. A few names crop up that might interest you. There's also some background stuff about the group's beliefs you might want to look at.'

Lean spent the evening looking at the pocket book. Despite his apparently harsh manner, he had been pleased with Robertson's find and had to admit to himself that it had evaded his earlier sweep of Powell's effects.

The handwriting was somewhat childish and the text littered with misspellings. What really intrigued him were a series of quotations from other texts, which provided some insight into the group's ideology. However, his eye was drawn to an entry in the back, which appeared to be of more recent date.

The Truth about God

Through the Old Testament, God perpetrated much that was evil, destroying thousands of his own helpless worshippers for comparatively minor offences (I Samuel 6:19). Christian commentators rarely accepted the Bible's own view of God as the originator of evil. Consider, for example, this quotation from Isaiah 45:7. 'I form the light and create darkness : I make peace, and create evil : I the Lord do all these things.' Thus God deliberately created the Devil before the beginning of the world because a pre-existing principle of evil was necessary to test the resolve of the human race. However, the Devil, not God, was the true creator of the earth and its creatures. Hence the magi prayed to Lucifer for assistance in all worldly endeavours and revered him as the ultimate source of their magical powers. The Christian Devil became a kind of composite of ancient gods in a polymorphous form. In the medieval period devil and devils were largely interchangeable. Lucifer was truly polytheistic and as God incarnated himself into an earthly body so the Devil would incarnate himself into earthly flesh shortly before Doomsday.

This demonic being was termed the Antichrist but we shall call him The Prince of the Morning Light. He was born in Babylon in 1599 where the Jews identified him as their Messiah. In the medieval period, no Christian was allowed to disbelieve in the Devil. Indeed the very idea of salvation depended on the existence of the Devil. Lucifer can, therefore, be seen as the *raison d' etre* of Christianity. We of the Brethren do not despise Christianity or deny its validity. We acknowledge the truth of its theology. We await the second coming, which is imminent.

Below this, in another weaker hand, were the words, 'Well developed Paul. I admire the clarity of your ideas. Suggest you bring this piece to the next meeting to share – MWS.'

Lean scrutinized the second hand carefully. He recognized it immediately.

Bottrell had no trouble finding Peter Koblinski. He was in the back of Boscean gallery, hard at work carving a six-foot high figure in yew. Koblinski, who wore headphones and was delivering hammer-like blows with his muscular arms, continued unaware of his visitor for some minutes as Bottrell inspected the contents of the studio.

There was a furious disorder about the room as if someone had opened the doors and let in a westerly storm wind. Piles of papers lay strewn across the table around half-empty coffee mugs, whilst the floor was covered in a mixture of wood shavings and discarded tools.

There was something suggestive of the satyr about the lean wild-eyed figure who laboured and sweated in front of him. With each stroke of the hammer and chisel, the profile of a head began to emerge and though the eyes were as yet sightless, the face was sharp and aquiline. There was something predatory and bird-like about it, he mused. No, this was not the man who had attacked him at the quoit. He was almost certain of it. Although powerful, this figure was much slighter and shorter.

At last Koblinski's struggle came to an end and, flinging down the hammer, he uttered a profanity, then turned in surprise to see Bottrell.

'Sorry – I had no idea.'

'That's OK, I was admiring the work.'

'That's an indulgence I never allow myself – at any rate not until this is finished.'

'May I ask what it is?'

'I'm calling it Resurrection, but there's nothing biblical about that. How can I help you, Mr Bottrell?'

'I've come to ask you about Anne Horrocks.'

'Ah, I see.' He wiped the surface of a stool clean with his sleeve and passed it to Bottrell. 'You were friends I gather. So Carmilla tells me. I'm sorry for your loss.'

'That's right, we were friends. I wanted to ask you about the group you both belonged to: The Brethren of The Morning Star.'

Koblinski passed a hand through his dark wet hair.

'You must understand that Anne was not a member of that group.'

'But you and Carmilla—?'

'Yes – we are Brethren. Have been for some two years and in case you are wondering – there's nothing sinister about the group. We all work with positive energy. Most of our rituals are to do with healing. Not that your colleagues in the police would believe us. Of course, we may be pagans but we don't perform human sacrifice, I told them so.' He laughed a high-pitched unnerving laugh, then rummaged on the table for a tobacco tin. From it he extracted a ready-made joint, which he proceeded to light.

'You want to know about the group? I'll tell you about it. We have nothing to hide. The Brethren started over in the States just after the war. It was an offshoot of a Crowleyan group and derived most of its ideas from Aleister's Abbey of Thelema period. The difference being that the Brethren eschewed most of his darker practices. We don't use drugs in our rituals for example and we practice sexual abstinence to heighten our powers.'

'So you're not Satanists?'

Koblinski laughed again, this time louder. The acrid smell of cannabis began to pervade the room.

'Satanists, do me a favour! We are dualists Mr Bottrell. We believe in both dark and light – the twin poles of the cosmos. We worship the Prince of the Morning Light – known by many names. You can call him Lucifer or whatever you like. The name is irrelevant. We think that you can draw on this energy, bring it into being to revitalize our own creativity and that of the natural world.'

'And you do this through ritual?'

'Yes, through ritual and meditation, and this part of the world is most powerful for that purpose. You're aware of the theory of ley lines I suppose?'

'Alfred Watkins?'

'And others since Watkins. The earth's surface is covered with an intricate network of energy lines and between these lines are what we call vortexes – points of power. Now, this western end of Cornwall has more of these channels than anywhere else in Britain and indeed more than most parts of western Europe – apart from Carnac in Northern France. We believe we can access these vortexes – much as ancient people in pagan times once did. It explains much in terms of folklore, for example, sightings of fairies, encounters with the Devil, apparitions of one kind or another. They can all be explained once you understand that theory. As I say there's nothing sinister about the work we do. We are beneficent in our motives.'

There was a long silence as Bottrell digested all this. Koblinski passed the joint to him and he inhaled deeply.

'OK, so what about Rebecca and Anne? How do you account for what happened to them?'

'We're as mystified as you are. They were good friends. Their loss impoverishes our lives. Whoever has done this doesn't share our aim – can't do. We believe in the celebration of life, not its termination. No one in our group would harm them. Am I making myself clear?'

Before he left the gallery, Bottrell shared the remainder of the joint. He asked Koblinski about the Exeter connection. He had recalled Slade but described him as something of an interloper whose ideas he had found distinctly oddball. According to Koblinski, he had not stayed long since it was rumoured he had placed unwelcome pressure on some of the group members. 'A weird cranky freemason with right-wing leanings. I always thought he was working for someone else,' was the comment he used to describe him.

He made his way up the gorse-lined path back in the direction of Lean's house. Overhead more storm clouds gathered, threatening rain. He quickened his pace, slightly giddy but also elated from the effects of the joint. He was thinking more clearly now. Anne, Rebecca, Paul Powell, Koblinski, all had discovered something of significance here at the end of the world, a way of accessing power. The ancients had known of it, but during centuries of Christianity that knowledge had been lost, buried under dogma and fear. He believed in Koblinski's account of the group. They were none of them capable of harming another human being but someone in this small, close community had discovered that secret and was willing to harness that power for his own occult purposes. Perhaps, the secret to that individual's identity lay in the very places Koblinski had described. He would return to the house and try to figure it out for himself.

He reached the house just as the heavens opened, finding it silent and deserted. A note on the kitchen table informed her husband that Hazel Lean had gone to Truro for the day and would be back around 6 p.m. After a brief foray into the drinks cabinet, where he found an unopened bottle of Glenfiddich, Bottrell poured himself a generous measure to assist his concentration and, glass in hand, made his way upstairs to his friend's study. The room, which consisted of a series of tall pine bookcases and a single white ash table housing a PC, surprised him. There must have been upwards of a thousand books here, ranging from the Latin classics to mythology, religion and medieval history. He had no idea that his friend's reading was so eclectic. He cast his eye along the medieval section. There were several books on the European witch craze, a leather-bound edition of Kramer and Springer's *Malleus Maleficarum* and a biography of the Elizabethan occultist Dr John Dee. It was curious, he reflected, that Robert had never revealed his interest to him in such matters. At the far end of the room he came upon a selection of maps and pulled out the OS map from the area. This he unfolded on the ash table. He noted that the map, which was well worn with constant use, had been drawn over with a series of pencil lines. Sucking on his pipe, he examined the lines carefully. Burns Down to Zennor Quoit. Zennor Quoit to Tol Pedn. He recalled the names and their folkloric significance. Koblinski was right in his assessment. He was certainly looking at a grid. At the end of each line lay a hill, a tumulus or site of antiquity, Bronze Age or Neolithic. Was it just coincidence? Was it really possible to harness that energy or was it just an elaborate fantasy on behalf of certain new age theorists? He was just folding up the map when he noticed the drawer of the ash table. Its key was protruding into his left leg. He hesitated for a moment, then opened the drawer where he observed a small purple-covered notebook, inscribed with the initials R.L. The contents were innocent enough: a series of jottings relating to meetings and colleagues in the job. However, this was not what made his heart race and his mouth dry. He examined the handwriting, then re-examined it. There could be little doubt of it. The long curled y's and Greek e's were identical in shape to those he had seen in Jane Wearne's diary. This was the other hand, which had described the details of the ritual of the initiation of the Brethren.

A sense of urgency overwhelmed him. He glanced round the room but there was little that might yield evidence save for a single wooden filing cabinet in the corner. He pulled at the drawers, but they were securely locked and he knew better than to force them open. His heart raced.

A noise broke the stillness. He went to the window and slightly but gently turned up the slats of the blind. From this angle he could see across the garden, past the rhododendron bushes to the yew grove, which partially obscured the old chapel. He was just in time to glimpse the back of Lean as he unpadlocked the door and entered. He was wearing a grey suit and carrying a holdall. Bottrell waited to see if he re-emerged, but there was no sign of him. He left the study, making sure that everything was as he had first encountered it, then made his way softly and stealthily down the staircase.

At the kitchen door he paused again and listened. Nothing, except the alarm call of the blackbird, broke the drowsy summer afternoon silence. He made his way rapidly down the lawn, skirting the bushes in case Lean should emerge and spot him. He felt remarkably clear-headed now. Maybe it was the adrenalin. He cursed himself for his dullness and slow-wittedness. All this time the key to the mystery of Thelema had been staring him in the face, yet he had been blind and deaf to its summons. It was clear now Anne Horrocks had died because she had got uncomfortably close to the truth. A similar fate had befallen Rebecca Wearne, although her murder had been constructed to look as if it was a ritual act. The absence of forensic traces suggested a professional approach and yet he had overlooked this most obvious of clues.

He was alongside the chapel wall now and drawing level with the window, which was obscured with white paint from the inside. He could hear some kind of meditation music playing from inside. For a moment he stood in silence not knowing what to do next. On no account should he confront Lean with his suspicions. Besides, he had no real evidence, nothing that would stand up in court. No. Best hold back, best bide his time, he would leave now and perhaps return to the chapel when Lean was back at work. He was just about to turn back to the house when the door swung open and Lean appeared at the threshold. He smiled at his old colleague and for an instant, Bottrell glimpsed the pupils of his eyes. They were like dark pin pricks.

'Were you looking for me?' he asked.

His tone was casual and friendly, as if Bottrell might have surprised him in the middle of a family barbeque. A waft of rich incense billowed out from the interior. Before Bottrell could utter a reply, Lean went on.

'You've not been inside my little sanctum before, have you, John? This is where Hazel and I like to come and relax. Why don't you come inside and we'll have a drink?'

For a moment Bottrell was disarmed by his familiar manner. Could this really be the man who had attacked him at the quoit, the person who had murdered two people? It didn't seem credible. Lean was a rationalist, a savant maybe, but no murderer.

He stepped inside. The interior was cool and dark after the bright July sunshine of the garden. He glanced round as Lean offered him a low stool, then poured him a tumbler of whisky. There was a strong masculine feel to the ambience. The walls were lined with ornate oriental tapestries showing pagan scenes in classical antiquity.

At the far end stood an altar built of granite. Upon it stood a large wooden image of a goat-like creature. Stained black, the statue carried a burning torch between its horns whilst a virile member curled up from between its powerful thighs. Below the figure, carved into a wooden plaque, were these words:

'Come unto me all ye who are desirous of me, and fill yourselves with my fruits. They that eat of me shall yet be hungry and they that drink of me shall yet be thirsty. He that obeyeth me shall never be confounded and they that work by me shall not do amiss.'

'I see you are admiring my little statue,' Lean said smiling. 'The words beneath it are from the Book of Ecclesiasticus. They are a homily to the Great Goddess.'

'I had no idea you were into this kind of thing.'

'Have been for years John – long before we met at police training college but it doesn't do to have unusual religious views if you're a copper.'

'I'm intrigued.'

'I can see you are.'

'No, I mean exactly how did you become interested in alternative spirituality?'

'Yes, that's the new age term for what I – we – believe. It started with Freemasonry really. I'm not sure how much you know about the background to masonry?'

'I was never a member.'

'I'd joined a local lodge while I was at the Yard but the revelation really came when I read *The Brotherhood*.'

'The Stephen Knight book?'

'Precisely. As you probably know, although masonry can be traced back only to the seventeenth century, its roots lie in something much more profound. It's connected to the Templars, the Gnostics and other groups that fell foul of the medieval churchmen.'

Lean was in his stride now and leaning back in the leather armchair as he waved his hands, developing his theme. Bottrell had never seen his old friend so animated or so lucid. It was a far cry from the automaton-like figure he had grown used to in his days at the Yard, the man who had read Wittgenstein and Marx at university.

'And what exactly are you now, a grand freemason?' he asked, noting that the whiskey had a rather sharp edge to it.

'Ah – that's a difficult question to answer. The journey has certainly been a long and interesting one. But what I've found here, John, in this far-flung end of the land is something remarkable, unique. It's become my turning point. I rather think you know what I'm talking about.'

'What do you mean, exactly?'

'You were always intuitive John, and despite your attempts to destroy your mind, during recent years, you've been rather successful in discovering quite a bit about our workings down here in the west. I have never underrated your intelligence.'

'You mean the Brethren?'

'Yes, the Brethren, although that organization is of course merely a vehicle for my higher purpose.'

'Which is?'

Lean raised himself from his chair rather unsteadily and stood in silence for a moment as he gazed at the figure on the altar.

'I refer to the Ascension. That's what I call it, John, though mere words are inadequate to express the wonder and power of the west. You see Crowley had it right. He had been here years ago and figured out what form the ritual might take. However, he was interrupted, distracted, you might say, by a woman. He lacked tenacity, you see, and he was already clouded by the heroin, which had by then become his habitual friend. I came here years ago with Hazel – long before I got the position in the force. I knew then that it was only a matter of cracking this code. You see this land forms a nexus of power. It's merely a matter of harnessing that power to bring the dark back into the light and thus to remove the stranglehold of centuries of Christian domination. When the Prince of the Morning Light comes again we shall all loosen our earthly chains. Then we shall not need drugs, religion or sex to act as props – not like Crowley. We shall see through different eyes, taste immortality, see the dead return again. That's what I mean by the Ascension and it's coming soon, John. Believe me. The rituals are almost complete. Tonight, Hazel and I will move now to a completion.'

He was talking fast with a kind of sustained, high-pitched fanatical edge to his voice. Bottrell, his senses already befuddled, sat down, then interrupted him.

'And Jane and Rebecca Wearne? And Anne Horrocks? Why did they have to die? What purpose did their deaths serve?'

Lean turned and shrugged his shoulders as if the deaths meant little to him or were an academic problem.

'They were regrettable. They were not meant to happen, I will admit that. Jane was an experiment. I had thought, like Slade at the time, that the path lay through ritual combined with sexual ecstasy – Crowley's idea, but it didn't work for me. I had thought Jane would be a willing participant, to be frank, but I made an error of judgement. I admit it. You see it would have been problematic had I allowed her to live. She was distressed, hysterical after the ritual. You must remember John that life is transient. What matters is not human kind but the work we achieve, the work, which is for the higher good. Sometimes sacrifices have to be made.'

'And the others, what about them?'

'They simply got too close to the truth. They were an annoyance, a distraction. Slade for example. He had intelligence but wanted the power for himself. I could not allow that.'

'What about the other members of the Brethren? Did they have any idea what you had done?'

Lean shook his head. 'They knew nothing about it. They, like others, have served their purpose. When you achieve the position and knowledge of a magus, John, you must not allow for distraction. It is a basic rule of procedure. Self-discipline is all. I'm sure you remember that from your training days.'

He paused and laughed. It was a short, hollow laugh that sent a chill down Bottrell's spine. He wanted to get out, to escape the presence of this crazed, arrogant figure who held forth in the small claustrophobic chapel, but his limbs would not allow him to stand up. He felt peculiar, disorientated, and it was not just the alcohol that caused his now overwhelming desire to sleep.

'I'm sorry, John,' the figure went on. 'As you know, I hold our friendship in high esteem, but I must say that you already know far too much for your own good.'

The words seemed distant as if he were listening to a discourse drifting in through an open window.

'When I spotted you in my study, I took the liberty of lacing your glass with a strong measure of henbane, thinking you might drop in to see me. It will be a fitting end, I assure you. The sad demise of a man consumed by grief for the untimely death of his beloved wife. But we have a little while left to us before the inevitable must be faced. Ask me any favour you wish.'

He had much to ask Lean. So many loose ends, so much to explain. But it was too late now. He had been an utter fool, he told himself. He had allowed Lean to lure him into his web and now he was stuck in its strands, powerless to act. He tried to open his mouth to say something, but the words would not come. His tongue stuck to his palate and his heart raced.

When he finally came to he realized he must have lost about half an hour. His eyes hurt, his heart pounded and he was gripped by nausea. He found himself sitting in the driver's seat of Lean's car and when he tried to move he discovered his hands had been tied with sealing tape behind his back. On the passenger seat next to him lay a half-empty bottle of malt whisky and the taste in his throat informed him that Lean had probably forced half of its contents down his throat. His captor was leaning over the driver's window, watching him as he slowly came to.

'I'm sorry it had to come to this but you've left me little option,' he said, smiling. 'However, I can assure you it will be a swift exit. It's coming up to high tide at the moment and we're on the highest part of the cliff. Is there anything you'd like me to do for you before we say farewell?'

Bottrell stared at the azure sky through the fly-stained window. For so long he had lived in the shadow of Frances' death but now he was faced with his own imminent demise it occurred to him that he had no desire to die, on the contrary, he possessed a keen appetite for life.

'I could do with a cigarette,' he suggested.

'We'll share one last smoke, then.'

Lean opened the passenger door and got in beside him. From the glove box he pulled out a fresh packet of cigarettes and unpeeled the cellophane with a measured meticulousness.

'It'll be like going into the West,' Lean said after a short silence. He lit two cigarettes, then placed one of them on Bottrell's lower lip. 'You know what the Romans called this land?'

Bottrell shook his head.

'The country of the setting sun from where no traveller returns. It's not a bad place to pass beyond the veil.'

Bottrell listened to the thunder of the waves as they crashed against the cliffs. From where he was sitting, he could see that the bonnet of the car was probably about three feet from the edge of the cliff. He knew this stretch of the coast only too well. It would be a sheer drop for him onto jagged rocks and death would be instant.

'I thought you might like to write a short valedictory note before you set off on your journey. I'm happy to dictate it for you,' Lean suggested. He reached into his jacket pocket and produced a small notebook and pen.

So that was it. A suicide note. Bottrell could hear Lean's testimony at the coroner's court even now. 'A good friend but unstable.

Depressed after the death of his wife. An alcoholic who could no longer face the world.'

'Perhaps you could untie my hands then,' he asked.

Lean produced a small pocket knife and began to cut through the tape.

Bottrell knew that he had only seconds to seize his chance. Suddenly the tape loosened about his wrist and with a quick but premeditated movement he brought his clenched fist up to engage with Lean's chin. For a moment the detective recoiled under the impact. The knife flew from his hand and ricocheted from the windscreen, the blade scoring Bottrell's cheek.

His left arm shot out and grabbed Bottrell by the throat. His eyes were red with anger now and he was snorting with a kind of demonic fury, but Bottrell had released the handbrake and the car rolled forward, quickly gaining momentum. In a second he had flung open the driver's door and hurled himself onto the cliff path in time to see the car lurch into a nose dive over the edge.

There was a glimpse of Lean's distorted figure clawing at the passenger door, the face fixed in a noiseless scream, a sound of falling boulders, then it slipped from view.

He lay on the grass, his head pounding. He was weeping now, the gulls screaming their litany above him, breathing great lungfuls of sea-scoured air until eventually he staggered to his feet, vomited again and the nausea passed. He peered over the cliff edge and could clearly see the crumpled outline of the car, half submerged beneath the waves, the front end concertinaed like a piece of tin. Some few feet away he spotted the half-burned cigarette he had been offered. Putting it to his lips, he drew on it deeply giving silent thanks to whatever deity had granted him the chance to live. He sat like this for a long while, his legs drawn up to his chin, listening to the slow roar of the sea on its strengthening tide, his face burning under the hot July sun. When at last he glanced down he could see nothing of the car. The grey blanket of the Atlantic ocean had enveloped it, erasing it from his consciousness. His soul felt light now, lighter than it had been for many years. He closed his eyes and sighed, not with weariness, but with relief. Soon he told himself, it would be sunset. And beyond sunset, there was the dawning of a new age.

He thought of Frances and for the first time in years he no longer felt that overwhelming sense of grief. He glanced ahead. She was standing some distance away on the cliff path. He could see her clearly; she was wearing the long green summer dress he had given her on their honeymoon, and she was smiling at him. He threw away the cigarette and smiled at her. Then the figure vanished from sight and he was left alone on the cliff edge. But he was not alone now. He would never be alone. He was sure of that.

Author's Note

While the locations in this novel are entirely real, the author wishes to point out that, with the exceptions of the characters of the late Aleister Crowley and D.H. Lawrence, all of the dramatis personae herein are entirely fictional and bear absolutely no resemblance to any persons living or dead.

Stone Dead is the first John Bottrell murder mystery novel.

Others in the series are:

Witch Jar – (Elliot Mackenzie Publishers)
Flowers of Evil (Elliot Mackenzie Publishers)
A Cromer Corpse (Contact Publishing)
All titles are currently available from www.oakmagicpublications.co.uk

Printed in Great Britain
by Amazon

86209763R00098